MOURNED BY MEN

QUEEN PENTHESILEA AND THE AMAZON WARRIORS AT TROY

KATIE FRENDREIS

This is a work of fiction. Names, characters, places, and incidents are products of the author's imagination or are used fictitiously and are not to be construed as real. Any resemblance to actual events, locations, organizations, or persons, living or dead, is entirely coincidental.

World Castle Publishing, LLC
Pensacola, Florida
Copyright © 2023 Katie Frendreis
Hardback ISBN: 9781960076946
Paperback ISBN: 9781960076953
eBook ISBN: 9781960076960
First Edition World Castle Publishing, LLC, December 12, 2023
http://www.worldcastlepublishing.com
Licensing Notes
Cover: Karen Fuller
Editor: Gwyneth Fullerton

To my mom, who encourages my nonsense
to Pen, who never lets me take myself seriously
and to Daisy, who walked through my stories and thought
they tasted good.

Chapter 1 - πρόλογος

PROLOGUE

Priam mourned his son just as I mourned my sister. Only Priam did not kill his son, did not plunge a bronze blade into his gut, did not feel his son's hot blood splash against his hand. The old king had shriveled since Hector's death—his murder— and sat upon his throne like an unburied corpse. I pitied him. He wore his grief like a pall. His bones protruded from his narrow body, poking through the paper-thin skin. Had no one made sure this old thing was eating? But I suppose a king cannot be ordered to do much of anything. And his grief was not foreign to me. Mine had created an ocean within me, tides of anguish that ebbed and flowed irregularly. Unlike the king, I had chosen a different path to follow in my pain.

The palace of Ilium smelled of sweat. Priam's advisors, sons, and generals lined the chamber, coughing and rustling as their king stared vaguely ahead. Ever since Hector's death, all of Ilium mourned. The chamber was ill-lit now, half its braziers dark. The grieving father found the colorful murals and painted arches of his own palace at odds with his despair and had ordered them painted over with black. Even Andromache, Hector's wife, had blanched at this—how could Ilium's finest art be erased because one king had lost a son? — and so the chamber was plunged into darkness so Priam would not be tempted to enjoy his surroundings.

At last, the king's glassy eyes regained their focus, and he found me kneeling before him. "Great queen," he wheezed, "Ilium is glad you have finally decided to join us in our war with the Argives."

I heard the unspoken slight. He wished my warriors had joined the battle before Hector was slain. Of course, I agreed with him. But my warriors had not, not until this late in the war, and so we arrived in time to mourn the loss of the city's favorite son. I heard my warrior's whispers. They hissed that I only wanted to help Ilium because I had once shared a bed with Hector. That I had loved him as a wife. They were wrong, all wrong, but there was no point in quelling rumors like those, not if it meant we would not come to Priam's aid now.

And Priam did need us. His city was dying around him, rotting like his son's corpse had as the monster had dragged it behind his chariot. And so I swallowed my injured pride at the king's words and bowed my head even lower.

"We pledge ourselves and our blades to your cause, great king." My words sounded hollow. Had I not promised my sister something similar? And had I not slaughtered her? Accident or not, she was now dead.

Someone at Priam's side snorted. I peered through the darkened chamber and saw one of his sons step forward. The swagger in the man's gait was unmistakable.

Paris. One of Priam's other sons. The architect of this whole war. I held back a snarl.

"Father, what can a handful of soft women do that our

warriors cannot? Have we not sent enough worthless fodder
to the Argives? Now we stoop to letting wet-nurses fight?"
He tossed his arrogant head, sending bronze curls cascading
over his shoulder.

So the pup wished to goad me.

I rose from my knees then, and I grinned as Paris
realized we were equal in height. Sweat had plastered my
own curls against my head, and dust clung to my cloak and
armor. I eyed the dandified princeling before me, took his
measure as his gorge rose and fell, and his mouth went dry.
I knew what reactions my appearance instilled in men. I had
seen such looks before. Looks that said, this little man still
fears me as he has feared no woman before, as he did during
our youth.

Silence strangled the hall as all eyes turned to us.

"You can insult my Amazons if you wish, little prince.
But remember, we have fought against the Argives before,
and we have won. How many battles have you won? And
I don't mean ones against the Argive whore you force into
bed each night." I could feel my palms begin to sweat, and I
clenched my fingers around the hilt of my sword.

The prince's eyes narrowed. He did not like to be
insulted by women, I remembered. "Maybe if you didn't have
your legs wrapped around your Amazon sluts, you could
have come here and saved our whole city by now!"

My sword was drawn before I even breathed. The
silence of the advisors and generals erupted into a cacophony
of argument and chatter. "I've come to help your pathetic city,"
I said, staring down the edge of my blade at Paris' quivering
face. "But if you think to insult my warriors to compensate for
your own failings, we can leave and let the Greeks tear down

Ilium's walls stone by stone."

Paris, to his credit, stood his ground, though it might have been from fear rather than composure.

"Enough!"

Priam's voice was stronger than his frail body would have me guess.

"Paris, get yourself out of this chamber before you offend every last ally we have!" The old man had risen from his throne and now stooped before it, his robes drawn around him in thick layers despite the oppressive heat. "Please, Queen Penthesilea, forget my son's ill-considered words."

I dropped my sword and slid it cleanly into its sheath, all without shifting my eyes from Paris. He gulped and, chastened like a scrappy dog, turned to bow to his father. Then he scurried back, the other men of the chamber surging from him as though he carried a disease. I watched him retreat from the hall. Poor Priam, to be left with a son like this and in such dire times as these. Hector, my old friend, had been well-loved for a reason. He would have ruled this city like a true king, like Priam. He could have made Ilium prosper.

If he hadn't been killed by the monster Achilles.

And if the city wasn't torn apart by war.

I looked over to King Priam. The old man settled into his throne once more, and I wondered if he would live to see the end of this war. Glancing at the faces of the men around him, I imagined they all had the same thought. Their king, already old, was now enfeebled further by grief. And their greatest hope for a successor decaying outside their enemy's tent.

Now Priam faced me with the barest hint of a gleam in his eyes. I could sense that his grief had turned momentarily to rage, as it must have done when he summoned me and my people. It was the same cold fury I had felt—still felt—since my sister's fateful death.

"You Amazons have always been friends of Ilium," intoned the king, sounding again like the mighty man I'd known. "Though you are late to join our cause, I welcome you openly now. All the gifts we promised will be yours as long as you uphold the promise you made me."

Inclining my head towards the noble king, I swore before all the leaders of Ilium.

"I swear, my lord, to kill Achilles."

Chapter 2 - πατέρας

FATHER

My mother told us our father was a god, but I think he was a man. A man who left us to perform great deeds and become a hero. But he left Otrera with Hippolyta and myself, and we thought little of him after that.

The soft sand beneath my feet, hot in the summer sunlight, filled my childhood. I ran with Hippolyta everywhere—fleeter than hares we were, chasing each other across our island home. Other women lived there too, some with children, some too old for it, but they all looked to Otrera for guidance. She had come from the western cities and knew how to run a community such as ours. And she was brave and fierce and strong, and so they looked at her almost as I did, like a great queen, though a queen of one small island only. We had no citadel nor large estate to call our own, only the small fields that fed us, the trees that shaded us, and the spring that slaked our thirst.

When I was but small, a man came to our island. He was not fearsome or warlike, only an older man with a limp and sadness in his brown eyes. His small boat slid upon our shores as I watched from a perch among the trees. The man climbed out, splashing awkwardly in the shallows, and heaved his boat further up the beach. Then he turned and headed straight for my mother's cabin. On his back was a large satchel which protruded in all manner of odd angles. Silently, I climbed down from my tree and followed the man, always staying back enough so he would not notice me.

"Rastor!" exclaimed my mother, rising from her work. She rushed out of our small home and met the man in the patch of garden just beyond the door.

For some reason, I hung back from them. I wanted to learn this man's purpose and thought my mother and he might conceal it if I made my presence known. So I stayed back, crouched in the shrubs on the far end of the garden.

The man, Rastor, returned my mother's greeting but not the cheerfulness of it. Instead, he sank to his knees in the dirt before Otrera.

"He's dead, my lady," was all Rastor said.

My mother, who I had seen cry over an injured sparrow but never a man, bit her lip and closed her eyes. Was she keeping back tears? Were tears meant to be chained like that?

After a moment, Rastor said, "I'm sorry." Then he brought out the satchel I had spied and laid it at my mother's feet. "These are his things." Together, they sat in the garden and arranged my dead father's possessions around them like children with their toys. Here was a sword wrapped in a shining bronze and leather sheath. A belt of woven gold. And the helmet. That was my favorite of all the riches Rastor brought us that day. It was a bronze cap with two metal segments that reached down the wearer's cheeks. A crest of red erupted from the crown like a tail. Had my father fought in this helmet? I wondered, cheeks turning red with excitement. Had he fallen honorably on the field of battle with this wondrous mane atop his noble brow?

Rastor also gave my mother several purses of coins as well as a handful of religious sigils. We had little use for gods other than our Moon Goddess here, but my mother thanked him all the same. She offered to let him stay the night in our home, but Rastor declined. Apparently, our island of women was not something he wanted to experience first-hand, and he said his good-byes and hurried back to his small boat and the wide sea and lands beyond.

After he left the garden, I rose from my hiding place and strode up to my mother. Tall for my age, I had to look down at her where she sat surrounded by my father's leavings. Tears glazed her eyes, but when she saw me, she gave a startled gasp.

"What was his name?" I asked. I could not mourn someone I'd never known, so no tears rolled down my cheeks.

My mother shook her head at my question, then looked anxiously about for my sister. "Do not speak of this," she said, her voice more tense and sad than I'd ever heard before. "Not to your sister. Please." She had never pleaded for anything of me. I did not understand at the time.

I plopped myself into the grass with her, my greedy hands reaching past the golden belt and the discarded amulets for the great bronze helmet. "Why not?" I said. The helmet was heavy in my small, childish hands.

Otrera took the helmet from my hands gently. "Your father was not a man," she said, firm now. I think she was trying to convince herself as much as me. "Your father was a god. He was the God of War. His godly blood flows in your veins, my dearest, yours and your sister's. That is why you are

so strong and why you fight like fierce little mountain cats."
She set aside the helmet then to tickle me, and I laughed and
screamed and forgot all about the man from the sea and his
strange gifts and stories.

Hippolyta ran home that evening, brighter than the sun,
golden-brown hair streaming behind herself in wild tangles,
both knees skinned but with a gap-toothed grin on her face.
My mother shot me a stern look when she skipped through
the doorway, but I said nothing, waiting for Otrera to speak.
Once Hippolyta settled, and we all supped heartily, mother
brought all the presents from the limping man.

"Lyta," she said, facing first my sister, then me, "Pen.
Neither of you have met your father, but today he has looked
down on us from Olympos to give us divine gifts." I kept my
mouth closed. I knew very well that the limping man had
been sent by no divinity, but I also knew my mother never
lied to us. "The gods have blessed us." She brought out the
helmet and the sword, the belt and the amulets. Hippolyta's
eyes grew wide as saucers. In the firelight of our small home,
the armor and weapons gleamed gold and bright. Again, my
gaze strayed to the helmet, and I saw Hippolyta turn to the
elegantly woven belt. She wiped her hands upon her shift
before reaching for the golden plaits.

"Mother, it's beautiful!" she exclaimed. Her voice was
filled with awe.

I picked up the helmet, and the division of "godly
gifts" was done. The sword stayed with our mother. She
spent the night regaling us with stories of the gods, how they
loved humans like herself on occasion, how they could rage

at each other and throw the heavens into deadly combat, how they created things we took for granted, trees, grass, fire. I, the younger of the children, fell into a haze of sleep and myth while Hippolyta asked my mother question after question about the gods who had made us, all the while clutching the golden belt in her grubby hands.

The island on which we lived was not small; certainly, it was larger than our small community needed, and there were many parts that we did not often go. One such region, a dense region of trees and ferns, was where Hippolyta and I found ourselves soon after the visit from Rastor. Hippolyta led the way as she always did, dodging through the tree limbs and nimbly leaping over twisting roots. Neither one of us had any chores that day and was not expected back home until much later.

"Look!" cried Hippolyta from ahead. I threw down the flower in my hand and followed her pointed finger. She had found a small gully, probably once a stream that had since dried out. The gully was mostly clear of trees and deadfalls, so we clambered down into it and continued our hike through its sandy discourse. Lyta was carrying on about something that only she understood when suddenly there was a tinge in the air.

I whistled for her to stop, and we both froze. I sniffed the air at the unfamiliar coppery, foul smell wafting towards us. At my side, Hippolyta tensed, smelling what I smelled. Ahead, the gully curved around a tall rock formation. With hesitating steps, we made our way up to the bend in the path. At the rock, we stopped again and strained our ears, but there was nothing but the sound of far-off ducks conversing noisily and the wind as it tossed through the tree canopy. I signaled for Hippolyta to stay behind me, and we two leaned out from behind the rock.

Just beyond the curve lay a shocking figure. It was the body of a man, his legs twisted awkwardly under himself, arms splayed out at his sides. My sister and I both gasped, but the man did not move. In fact, his chest did not even rise and fall with breath. He was dead. We came closer and saw why. His leather cuirass had been torn straight through, past flesh and down to the bone in several places. He looked to have tried to defend himself as his forearms were similarly shredded. One hand still clutched a short dagger, which was coated in blood. A cap of leather had tumbled from his head and lay discarded a few paces away. When we got closer, we saw his face had gone purple and green from the summer heat, bloating in spots like a balloon. His skin, whatever shade it had been in life, was unrecognizable now. The dead leaves and dirt under his body were soaked through with the dried brown of his lifeblood.

Hippolyta drew away from me and stared into his mottled, rotting face. I turned from it in disgust. The man's blade came into view, and I bent down to pry it from his fingers. Blood had dried along the sword's edge, coating the crosspiece. I turned it over and found a tuft of fur stuck amid the dried blood. This seemed significant, and I determined then to show it to mother.

I looked over my shoulder at my sister and found her still staring at the corpse's hideous visage. "Come," I said. "We must tell Mother of this." She nodded, but did not look up, so strangely focused on the man's face. Something in her gaze put fear in me, for I had never seen her look so at another being before. What was it she saw in the dead man? Why did she not wish to turn away from so awful a sight?

At last, with a tug of her hand and a nervous whimper, I was able to turn her from the corpse, and we scampered back towards Mother, towards our village, away from unblinking death and scattered remains.

Mother's eyes flared like flames when we told her breathlessly what we had seen in the woods. A man, firstly, one armed and sneaking across our island. Secondly, some other hunter, perhaps not human, and one that could shred armor like so much parchment. She gathered together the women of the island and had us recount our tale. I showed them the man's dagger with blood and fur on it. Many of them agreed with Otrera and discussed sending out scouts to the uninhabited portions of the island the following day while planning to set bonfires and torches near their homes to keep away intruders in the night.

Only one woman scoffed at our worries. Agathe was her name. She had once lived in the cities with men, only coming to our island after falling pregnant without a husband. Our island had no use for weddings or husbands, and so she had fled to us when her father and mother threw her out of their home and threatened to beat her. Poor Agathe was still young, her infant son still feeding from her breast, and she did not know truly the wild ways of the world out here. We may have been safe from angry fathers, but there were more concerns in the world than that. But Agathe did not fear the mysterious threat like the others, and no strong words or invocations of our Moon Goddess from my mother could convince her otherwise.

So at nightfall, when each of us returned to our homes and set fire to blazes at our doors and kept any weapons close at hand, Agathe fed her babe and slipped off to sleep in her home at the edge of our settlement without lighting a single torch.

Throughout the night, my dreams disturbed me, and I found comfort in wrapping my small fingers around the curved edges of my father's bronze helmet. Sometimes I woke and would notice my mother sitting between me and my sister, her hands on the sword Rastor had given her. I did not know yet how well she could handle such a blade. But though my mother sat ready to defend us with her life, no threat came knocking at our door that night. When finally the sun rose and we stepped into the garden, I sighed. Surely if our home had been ignored in the night, so must all the others' homes have been.

But I was wrong.

Agathe, from the other end of the village, let up a cry such as I had never heard before. Before she could go on, her own anguish strangled the sound. My mother rushed over, through our garden and the intervening woods, past the other homes, to where Agathe knelt before her own cottage. I raced after my mother, Hippolyta, my fleet-footed shadow, as always.

"Agathe," said Otrera, kneeling beside the other woman. Women from other homes filtered over to see why she had cried out so. "Agathe, what is wrong?"

Agathe held up a torn bit of blanket, soaked through with blood.

"My son!" she cried, her voice already hoarse. "My son!"

Chapter 3 - πόλεμος

THE WAR

The generals of Priam wanted my Amazons to throw ourselves headlong into battle with the Argives with no thought to strategy or careful plotting. But what did they know? They had been losing a siege for almost ten years. I ignored them and climbed the never ending stairs to the top of Ilium's battlements. Some of the men with me wheezed and coughed at the exertion. No wonder they could not beat the Argives. These men had grown weak since I had last been here, what seemed like another lifetime ago.

My sister had been there too, and Hector. And Paris had seemed not quite so foolish as the lovestruck man who had started a war.

But none of that mattered now.

My warriors had stayed off the walls. As I mounted yet another stone step, I pondered at the city's inability to trust women warriors, though they had set much of their hopes on our slim shoulders. One warrior woman on the walls would be enough; they did not need to see more of us arrayed in our battle-hardened armor. I had left off my armor as it was, wearing only the familiar leopard skin at my back and short chiton, like the ones worn by the generals and princes beside me. It was too hot for more than that, although, of course, I wore my sword at my belt. Though I was among allies, I knew better than to trust so many rough, war-angered men.

Priam met me at the top of the wall, along with the searing blaze of the summer sun. Dust rose in great clouds from the churning killing-ground at the foot of the walls, sending curtains of haze high into the sky, almost as high as the impenetrable walls of Ilium. The king inclined his wizened head to me, a meeting of equals.

His wife, Hecuba, stood at the edge of the battlements. Younger than Priam but still wrinkled with age and sorrow, she rested her hands against the stone balustrade, peering out at the plain before the city. Once a lush, grassy meadow leading down to the long beaches below, the greenery had been churned away by boots and sandals, hooves and chariot wheels. All had been stained with the blood of those killed in the long war.

I stepped to the edge of the wall and looked down. Where had the great Hector been killed? Was it there, by the destroyed stump of a once-great tree? Or further down, where scavenger birds tore apart some poor, forgotten foot soldier's corpse?

Would I meet my own death somewhere down on the killing fields?

The deep chasm of grief yawned within me then, making me wish for a quick death. The suffering would only stop after my own life was taken. I could march outside these thick walls, armed with nothing but my sadness, and let some lucky Argive strike me down. He could count a queen among his death tally, and I could finally be at peace.

Suddenly, another figure on the wall caught my attention and pulled me from my dreams of death. Clad in black, the young widow of Hector joined me at the edge. Andromache was her name. I knew of her. She was beautiful, as Hector had been, but her face was lined now with tears, her soft eyes rimmed with red instead of kohl, her hair pinned haphazardly around her crown instead of curled and twisted to perfection. Here was another broken soul, like Priam and myself.

But not like us. The sun glinted off the bits of gold jewelry at her neck and wrists. And I stared at her. She was breathtaking in the glory of early morning, despite all the sadness that clung to her like mist. The world had taken her husband from her, yet still, she held her chin high as though that small defiant act might change the fate of this doomed city. But no, Andromache was not like me, nor was she like Priam. She had lost her beloved husband, as we had lost sister and son, but her hand had not thrust the sword nor wielded the scepter of a king. No part of Hector's death had been her fault. If rumors could be trusted, the woman had begged her husband not to fight Achilles.

But I had led my warriors to battle against Theseus. I had forced Hippolyta to join us, though she never stopped loving the wretched king of Athens, and I had endangered his life and caused her to defend him. And Priam had let Hector fight — not just his son, but a whole city! — because Paris and Helen refused to concede their little farce of love.

"It was there," said Andromache, her voice low, almost a whisper. She pointed to the narrow gates of Ilium, not far from our position on the city's wall. "He stood against Achilles and made to charge, sword in hand, but Achilles had a spear and...." Her voice faltered. "He was a good man," she added at last.

I nodded and looked away from the widow, not wishing to see the tears that flowed fresh down her cheeks. "I knew him when he was a lad," I said, hesitating. Surely, this woman had heard the rumors about Hector and me, and I had no wish to cause her further suffering. But I continued anyway. "He was the most honorable fighter I ever knew. He was fair and strong and brighter than the full moon." How I wished to see his smiling face one last time! "And he would do anything to protect those he loved, even if it meant dying for his city. And his family."

From the corner of my eye, I saw Andromache bite down on her trembling lip. "I wish this war would end." All the bitterness, the weariness of a lifetime of fighting filled her slender form. "This city has stood for so long, unchallenged. But now we live our every day in fear. It isn't right." She clenched her fists. "I wish I could do something."

"You would make a good warrior," I said.

That astonished her, and she turned to me sharply.

I smiled at her and said, "You are fierce as any fighter, and you care about your family. If you were a man, you would be out there too, defending Ilium with your life and your sword."

Andromache frowned. "If I were a man, I would never have let this absurd war drag on so long. Ilium is doomed. Now we simply prolong what is inevitable."

"That may be true." I knew she was right. There was very little hope for this city, for these people. I already knew now that my Amazons would not be enough to stem this tide. I would try to slay Achilles, but though great and ferocious, he was only one man in a sea of Argive warriors. Was I dooming my own warriors by joining this battle?

At that moment, Priam decided it was time to discuss military matters. He moved away from his wife and gestured to the assembled generals, who swelled around him like bees in a hive. Andromache lowered her gaze and drifted off to join Hecuba, two women brushed aside now that plans were to be made. How different I was from them to be included in this man's talk. But how similar as the men sneered down their noses at me, how they smirked when they thought I did not see them, how they spoke of me and my women as if our ears could not hear. At least they had some fear of me, and it kept them just far enough away so my blade could not swipe off any roving hands or ill-considered gestures. I would rather have them fear me than ignore me as they did Hecuba and Andromache. I would rather have them bow to me than call me a whore like they did Helen.

The women gone, we warlords looked out over the battlefield. One of them pointed out the camp of the Argives, though it was clear enough who lived in the overflowing tents encamped along the vista of beaches to the west. The morning was still young, and the men from the enemy camp had not yet ridden out against our city. According to the generals, this would start soon.

Priam tensed as the Argives began to chant, their voices raised in bone-chilling cheers. One among them moved. The armored figure strode along the edges of the camp until he reached a gleaming chariot pulled by two white horses. Taking no second rider in the chariot, the man whipped his horses into action, and they emerged from the Argive camp like dolphins from the sea. Something dragged behind his chariot.

The old king paled, though surely he had watched this sight many times by now. Farther down along the wall, Hecuba and Andromache sagged into each other, though still, they watched. Some of the king's advisors turned away. So these women were not so weak as all that.

The chariot drew closer to Ilium's walls, and the thing that dragged behind it resolved itself into what we all expected—Hector's body. Achilles had strung rope through Hector's bare ankles, and the corpse's arms flopped behind it. The dead hero's face stared blindly up towards the yellow sun.

The men in the enemy camp gave up a loud roar as Achilles neared Ilium. Along the walls, men and women watched in silence as their prince's corpse was tossed like a sack behind the monster's chariot, flung about in the dust and the dirt without a shred of reverence. Only I, standing fresh to this indecent sight, snarled wolf-like and clenched my fist around the hilt of my sword.

Achilles rode closer, almost within bowshot of the walls. My fingers itched for my bow, the curved wood I myself had fashioned, dreamt of letting one single arrow fly into Achilles' muscular neck and slaughtering this arrogant beast of a man. Once he reached his chosen distance, the Argive wheeled his horses so they rode parallel to the walls. He slowed them to a trot and turned his face to those of us standing atop the battlements. None of us could see his face through the ebony glint of his helmet, but I imagined dark eyes gleaming up at us with hate and fury like an evil monster from legend.

I could tell this ritual had occurred many times before my arrival. How irreligious and disrespectful could these

Argives be if they let this man perform such vile acts on an enemy corpse? How could the kings of the Argives allow this? How could the camped men cheer on their monstrous hero? And how could Achilles live with his own dishonor?

Finally, the sight of her son's broken corpse brought out a little scream of pain from Hecuba. Andromache clutched the sobbing queen in her arms, and the two clung to each other. None of the men, not even Priam, went to them. The king remained staring out over the battlements, watching his dead son get dragged through the dust. Hector's slayer stared back, a demon in armor without any honor and with the blood of princes on his hands.

Then the killer shouted to us, and his voice was clear over the wind and the rattle of his chariot harness, "Send out your soldiers, Ilium, so that I may have more corpses to decorate my chariot."

My fists clenched so hard they hurt. Had I been out there on the sands with him, I would have ripped out his throat with my bare hands. But I was on the wall with the king, destined only to watch the tactics of the Argives this day. Below us, the gates creaked open, and Ilium's chariots rode out in defense of the city. At this, I let myself smile. Ilium would defend itself today, and the city would defend Hector's corpse forever.

Achilles had already turned his own chariot, thrown back his head to laugh as he thundered back to the massing Argives. He would not be killed this day. I knew that for certain. His hubris glowed about him like a shield—maybe his mother really was a goddess, as some claimed. But I knew that, while not today, the Argive beast could be killed. I had sent enough men to their tombs who thought themselves invincible. All men can die. And so would Achilles.

The chariots of Ilium drove forwards just as the Argives' own spurred to meet them. Behind the chariots, both sides sent up several ranks of infantry, lightly harnessed foot soldiers to wade in after the rumbling chariots. Unlike my Amazon forces, none of the fighters here rode on horseback, and the men churned the sand and dirt with their own sandalled feet as they charged. From both sides, archers in the chariots rained iron-tipped arrows into their opposition. Men toppled, men screamed, and men writhed as the pain of the swift darts sent them to the ground to be trampled by following chariots. Blood fell to the sand, sizzling in the heat.

By the time the chariot lines clashed, Achilles had turned again and dismounted. He gripped a gleaming spear in one hand and a fearsome shield in the other and charged the men of Ilium. His Argive allies parted before him, and he let loose his wrath upon the men of Priam's city. Archers took aim at him, but always he diverted their arrows against his gold-colored shield. Some proud men, wishing to make themselves legendary, stood against him, but his swift spear thrust at them, finding the chinks in the armor, tearing through their soft bodies, leaving them forgotten upon the sands.

All eyes atop the walls fixated on the monster below.

"Only Hector could equal him," breathed one man, too old to join the fighting and too cowardly to try.

"Maybe among men," I countered. No one looked at me, but I could tell none believed my boast.

No, not a boast. A threat.

Tomorrow my Amazons would ride against the Argives, and we would see who would win that battle.

Hours later, when the setting sun shaded the sky purple, I approached the Skaian Gates. Others stood with me, feeling the hot sand through our sandals—men whose jobs it was to collect the dead from the field of battle. Above us, in the walls, teams of men cranked the massive gates open with much sweat and strength. These gates had stayed sealed against the invaders for ten years, only opening for Ilium's forces. I stared up at the gargantuan doors as they swung open and felt a breeze strike my face. The air within the citadel had been stifling and still, but from beyond came the cool breeze off the sea.

The corpse-collectors trudged ahead of me, dragging their empty wagons behind them. I held my breath for a moment, waited, then strode to join them on the killing field. Now I wore all my armor, my helmet pushed back from my brow like the other men, but still, I had the leopard skin wrapped over my shoulders. I wanted to stand out to any watching Argives.

I watched the corpse-men go about their business with silent alacrity. There was a feeling on the battlefield, an aura that made words seem inappropriate. As several of them worked to separate bodies whose limbs had become tangled, I ambled past the other dead. To my right lay a youth, newly-bearded. Both his wrists had been hacked through, and a deep gash in his chest had probably killed him. His eyes were scrunched shut as though he had squeezed them tight in his final moments so as not to see death coming. On my left, a grizzled, older warrior lay face down in the sand. A spear head protruded from his lower back, having torn through his

poorly-fashioned cuirass. Not far off lay the corpse of a horse,
a great dark stallion. Spikes from an opposing chariot wheel
appeared to have torn through its legs and sent it down to
bleed to death.

All this death, all these nameless corpses, brought my
sister to mind. Her graying face, her bloodstained chiton,
her lips parted with the whisper of unspoken words. I saw
Hippolyta lying in the sand under the remains of a shattered
chariot. There she was again, an arrow piercing her shoulder
and another deep in her gut. For a moment, I thought I might
cry, even imagined the sting of tears against my cheeks. But
nothing came. No tears fell, no breath hitched in my throat.
How was it that I could see so many dead Hippolytas and feel
nothing?

But the empty chasm in my chest did not surge this
time with sadness or fear or loss. It remained cold and dark
and empty.

When the men were done loading corpses into their
wagons and turned back to great Ilium, I knelt in the sands,
pushing my fingers into the sifting grains. These were the
sands on which I would die. Or where I would slay Achilles.
Then the gods would be at peace, and the death of my sister
would be balanced out in the heavens.

For a time, I knelt alone. I could sense men from the
Argives' camp watching me, but I did not meet their gaze.
Then, their eyes still upon me, I unslung my bow, pulled an
arrow from their quiver at my hip, and drew. They tensed,
thinking I meant to break the nightly truce and shed their
blood. But I drew back and aimed my arrow skywards, then
released. The slim shaft flew into the sky, arcing gently as it
ran out of momentum. I stared directly ahead at the watching

Argives. Their eyes followed the curve of the arrow, staring as it finally reached its apex and began its descent. Still, I watched them and not the arrow.

Finally, the iron arrowhead drove itself into the sand, not two paces from where I stood. The shaft was buried halfway up its length.

"Argives!" I shouted. "The next one is for Achilles."

Then I turned and strode back to the gates of Ilium.

Chapter 4 - λεοπάρδαλη

THE LEOPARD

Our village mourned Agathe's son while also planning a hunt. My mother stepped into the other woman's hut, saw the scraps of bedding by the babe's crib and blood and hair within the home and a trail leading into the forest, and knew some beast had killed the boy. Agathe sat like a rock on the edge of the village well, women clustered around her, taking turns holding her hands and rubbing her shoulders. But the poor mother's eyes saw nothing, and her limbs felt no comfort from their welcome touches. After the first moments of shock and frenzy had worn off, she quieted to an almost deathly stillness.

I had never seen such grief before. My mother had learned of my father's death, true, but her pain had been tempered by distance and acceptance. Agathe felt no such comfort. She gazed blankly past the women trying to hold her and saw the clearing where her baby had toddled on unsteady legs only yesterday. She saw the other children of the village gathered together a few paces off, and she knew her son would never again play their games nor learn to run and climb and spar like them. She looked so still that I feared she had died as well.

Slipping my hand into Hippolyta's, we stalked to Agathe's hut at the edge of the village. Our mother stood almost at the forest's edge, her hands hovering over blood-spattered leaves. Though she looked calm, I saw the tracks of several tears lining her cheeks. Hippolyta and I stared at her, wide-eyed, innocent until now of the realities of the world.

"Is he dead?" Hippolyta asked. Her lower lip quivered as she spoke.

Otrera nodded. "A beast came and took him in the night. The torches warned it away from the other homes, but it found easy prey here." She sucked in a deep breath. "I must gather the strongest hunters. We cannot let such a dangerous creature roam free on our island." With that, she swept from us and into the crowd of women who awaited her commands.

"We should help find it," said Hippolyta. She had stopped crying, and she jutted out her chin like some heroic statue. "We're as good hunters as any."

I nodded, though I thought to myself that hunting small game was very different from this mystery beast. If Hippolyta was going to be fierce and brave, then I, too, must be so. As our mother and the other women planned their hunt, the two of us rushed back into our home and gathered up the homemade spears from our corner. Hippolyta wrapped her new golden belt about her waist, and I placed the helmet on my brow. Of course, it was too big, and it slid comically down until all I could see was the bronze of the inner crown. I tugged off the helmet and set it down on my bed. Someday, I would wear it, I thought, but not today. The sword Rastor had brought lay nearby, and I plucked that up instead. Too heavy, it sank immediately to the floor. Again, I set down my chosen item, vowing to use it someday.

The little dagger I had found in the dead man's hand was hidden below my cot, and, recalling it, I grabbed the small blade in a flash. It had none of the flair of the well-crafted sword of my father, but its edges were keen, and the handle sat well in my grip.

Thus armed, we returned to our mother only to find her and the other hunters about to leave the village. She saw us instantly and shook her head. "You two must stay here with the others and protect the village while we are gone."

The village did not normally have assigned guards, and I knew Mother was putting us off. "No!" Hippolyta stamped her small foot on the hard-packed earth. "We found the dead man! And we can hunt with you." I nodded my agreement.

Our mother still forbade us from going. "Promise me by the Moon Goddess that you will do as I say." At that, we could not argue and watched sullenly as the company took up arms and ventured into the woods beyond our small homestead.

The air grew hot as midday neared, and still, none of the hunters returned. Hippolyta and I took turns casting our makeshift spears into the dirt, competing over whose went farthest and how deep each dug into the ground. So far, my sister's throws were longer, but mine went deeper.

"How long will it take?" grumbled Hippolyta. Boredom did not sit well with her, and I could see her beginning to challenge our mother's command to remain in the village.

I shrugged. I had only ever hunted grouse before. How could I predict how long it might take to slay such a predator? "Probably until nightfall."

My sister jogged over to pick up her discarded spear.

She hefted the wooden stick in her hand and chewed on her lower lip. I recognized the look on her face.

"But Mother said to stay here!" I cried.

Hippolyta looked at me and shook her head. "She told us to protect the village. If we go and kill this monster, then we'll be following her orders." She tossed her curls and stared at me, exasperated, wondering why I could not just do what she told me. But hadn't Mother also commanded us to stay in the village while we protect it? As usual, Hippolyta chose which rules to follow and which to ignore.

And as usual, I followed my sister. With the sinking weight of guilty disobedience churning my belly, we picked up our spears and scampered through the loose wending of homes that made up the village. At the outskirts of town, where the forest encroached with eager, reaching branches, Hippolyta halted. She sucked in a deep breath, furrowed her brow, then raced on into the woods. I followed at her heels, not sure whose disappointment would sting more, hers or mother's. So I raced through the ferns and deadfall with my sister, leaving the small village far at our backs. We ran until our lungs grew tight, until the sweat poured down our faces and our muscles ached. Once or twice, I caught a glimpse of a lone hunter from my mother's group crouched in some underbrush or stalking through a sunlit clearing. But we flew past them far enough where I assumed they could not catch sight of our fleet heels. Hippolyta called a halt at a small stream that trickled along that part of the island, and we drank greedily.

Hippolyta decided we ought to become methodical in our hunt. First, we circled our quadrant of the island, searching the ground for marks or spoor of the beast. Then, we climbed some of the taller trees and surveyed the land from above. We found nothing. The great cat, whatever it was, remained hidden from us. I recalled our mother's teachings, how she told us that these predatory felines had the stealth of a ghost in the dark. I was about to remind my sister of this fact when she cut the air with her free arm, silencing me at once.

Below our tree slunk the biggest cat I had ever seen. Four muscular legs strode lithely across the forest floor, its body undulating with every step. I stared down at it, gape-mouthed, mesmerized by the play of sunlight across its yellow and black speckled fur. As it crossed beneath the overhanging arm of a tree, shadow and light dappled the beast and made it almost invisible against the ground.

In the tree branches below me, Hippolyta's breath hitched. She had been in the process of climbing back down to the ground but now froze at the sight of the great predator. My own breath caught, and my mouth went dry. Could the beast climb? Would it see or smell us? I suddenly realized I knew so little of such creatures. Why had I ever thought Hippolyta and I might bring down something so, so splendidly awful?

The cat pulled its lips back in a bleak interpretation of a grin. Its tongue slid out of its slavering maw and ran along the edges of its sharpened fangs. I tried to hold back a shudder lest the leaves around me shiver as well. I dared not even move my head enough to see Hippolyta more clearly. I hoped with all my heart that she would remain still. Surely, she would sense the severity of our situation as well as I.

It seemed the cat might glide away from us without incident.

But then a hiss of a sob escaped Lyta's lips, and a thin trickle of urine crept down her leg to dribble the length of the tree. The cat curled in on itself at the pungent smell of my sister's fear. It turned its golden eyes upwards. We three were locked together in terror, hunger, drama, and the hunt. Beneath the tawny fur, muscles rippled and contracted like bundles of watchful snakes.

I shivered.

Hippolyta lost her grip on the branches.

The cat sprung upwards as though it might have just gained the ability to fly.

I reached for the little knife I had found by the dead man.

Hippolyta screamed.

Somehow, she and the cat met in a tangle of brambles and dirt just below the tree. My sister tried to reach for her spear, which she had rested up against the trunk before we climbed up. How silly that seemed now! Just us two, hunting this massive creature made of claws and teeth! In any case, the weapon was too far from her, and the cat sank its fangs into her reaching arm. She exploded with sobs and pain.

My sister. My Lyta. She would die like that bloated man from the gully. I would be alone.

Her screams tore through the woods, but I doubted anyone from my mother's hunting party would come in time. There was only me.

Dagger clenched tightly in my sweaty hand, I dropped from my place amidst the branches. For a moment, I could not see, and I was met with the dust of the ground, the twisted brambles scratching and scraping against me, and the hot, animal smell of the cat. I felt the heat from its furred, muscular body, heat that rolled off in waves as though the thing were a lit hearth fire. How alive this beast was!

I blinked and struck out with my little knife. Poor Hippolyta cried out as flesh was torn from bone by the cat's teeth. Then my blade thunked into fur and muscle and bone. The cat let go of Lyta and hissed with shock. It couldn't be pain. My knife couldn't have hurt it that much. Shocked, though, I tore out the blade. Hot blood poured from the haunch, darkening the fur and spilling onto the dirt and my own body. Where it touched me, it felt so hot, almost like steam. A noise escaped me, but I was reaching forwards now, trusty blade ready. I stabbed against the creature's deep chest, between ribs, into some meaty, bloody bits within. Whatever my blade touched must have been vital, for the cat shuddered and jogged a step or two away.

Lyta bled and wailed and writhed in her patch of dirt.

I flew at the cat and stabbed it again and again, now in the armpit, now in the throat. There, the blood flowed unstoppably, like a river, gushing over me and Hippolyta and the cat. Then, the fiery look of murder left its eyes. One more thrust of the blade, and the cat was still.

I looked down at myself, covered in the cat's blood, and Lyta, dripping with her own, shuddering because of her own pain, her eyes glazed and unfocused. I hated the sight of the cat's body, hulking beside us, still as a mountain. I hated the blood that coated me like a cloak.

And so I cried out for mother, for dear mother, to come and help us poor, silly children.

Otrera and her fellow hunters found us shortly after, drawn by the deathly screams of both us and the cat. Mother made sure Hippolyta's wound was dressed tightly before she was carried back to our village. She stared at me longer after the other women had gone, eyes flitting between me and the dead animal at my side.

Finally, she spoke. "You took a life." Her words floated down to me and pushed through the dried blood that muddled my hearing. "Do you feel pleasure in this?"

I shook my head, tears still dripping down my face. "No," I sobbed. "It was horrible." I wanted to look away from the dead cat but found I couldn't. How did men go to war and kill other men and then go on living afterwards? My small body quaked at the thought. This cat was enough, I told myself. I could never kill again.

Mother's eyes stared deeply into mine, ferreting out the truth in my answers. When she saw what she liked, she took me up into her arms, blood and all, and carried me home.

The village was subdued upon our arrival. Of course, there was still the pall of Agathe's babe's death. And now Hippolyta and her wound. Many of the women had never seen such a wound. Or they had and knew the odds one had of surviving it. And so the celebration of my hand in killing the beast that terrorized us was tempered and quiet. That was just as well. Mother smuggled me into our own home with less fanfare than I imagined possible.

But I knew what I'd done. I saw the golden fire drain from the cat's eyes when I closed my own. I had done that. I had killed it. I had killed, just as the beast had.

Perhaps as my father had.

A God of War must have killed many times. But I, wrapped in bedclothes and placed beside the hearth, found no revels in my kill, like gods would. It was only after some hours that I realized the bloody dagger still rested in my curled fingers. I flung it away, heard it clatter against the hearthstone, as I squeezed shut my eyes and listened to the whimpers of pain coming from Hippolyta as the village women tried their hands at healing her.

Chapter 5 - πόλεμος

THE WAR

I flung the leopard skin over a low couch in the antechamber to my rooms in Ilium's palace. My blood was up, and I could not calm my thoughts. All I could see when I closed my eyes was the body of Hector lolling carelessly at the back of Achilles' chariot. Achilles had no right!

For a flash, I imagined he had been wearing a leopard skin over his shoulders while he rode, but I blinked my eyes, and it was gone. No, he had worn only armor and shame, not my pelt. I snarled at no one and stalked across the room to where some servant had set an amphora of watered-down wine. Pouring some for myself, I drank deeply, but the sweet taste did little to steady my nerves.

A soft knock came then on my chamber door, and I spun, ready to pounce on whoever dared intrude on my night. But it was only a woman, her head bowed low like a servant. She shuffled into my chamber, keeping her head down, until she reached the glow of the lantern-light when she raised herself up to her full height.

All breath left my body. As she stood in the lamplight, the soft orange glow of it wrapping around her well-formed shape, she reminded me of my mother's stories of the Moon Goddess—a creature made of beauty and air and light. Golden hair curled around her creamy shoulders. Pink lips parted dreamily. Her eyes—her eyes were curious, a color indescribable, and round like shields.

But she was sad. Her brow furrowed slightly, and the barest hint of wrinkles creased the edges of her eyes and mouth.

That was what ten years of war would do to you.

"So you're Menelaus' wife?" I asked. She was still beautiful, but, I reminded myself, only a human.

The golden beauty before me turned away towards the flame then. "I was once the wife of King Menelaus," she answered. Her voice was held together by webs of strength that had probably been threatened and broken down over the years in Ilium. "I came to Ilium as the wife of Paris."

Her tone rankled me. I saw past her beauty then and saw Hector lying dead in the sand. She had killed him just as much as Achilles had, for she had brought this war upon Priam's people. Something in my eye or brow revealed my thoughts to her, and she unconsciously took a step back.

"Why must I be someone's wife?" said Helen. Now she sounded defeated, her voice soft and thin. Perhaps she had expected sympathy from a woman like me, but I had no sympathy left. It had died with Hippolyta. She continued, "Why can I not be myself without some man to give me purpose?"

"Did you not choose to wed these men?" I asked. "Did you not choose to run away from your husband and bring war to Ilium?" My rage at Achilles was spilling over onto Helen, and I strode forward at her as I spoke. She shrank as I did so.

"Did you not see Priam throw his soldiers onto the plains and watch them die but stay here with your lover? Though you knew you could stop it all?"

Did I not know I could have saved Hippolyta by not raising my sword? That she could still be beside me had I not rushed off to violence as I always did? That Hippolyta and I could grow old on our island with our friends and die, not in combat but in peace?

Helen let out a little sob. I realized what I must look like, striding like some avenging warrior, eyes full of hate. But how could I hate someone I had never met?

"Queen Penthesilea," she said, sinking to her knees on the cold floor, "have you ever loved someone so deeply that you would suffer all for him?"

I stared at her and considered her question. Of course, I had loved. I loved my sister, and my mother, and the women of our island. But no, I had not loved the way she meant. Whatever kind of love she had with Paris. I held back a sneer. How could anyone love such a repulsive worm as Paris?

But I shook my head at her.

"I—when I was in Sparta, Menelaus thought he loved me. But he did not. He worshiped me so that his friends would become jealous of him. He lavished me with gifts so that his people would think our love godlike. But his love had only to do with him. I could have been anyone for all he cared. And then—then, when Paris came. I thought—I thought that he saw me. That he saw the trappings Menelaus had set around me, and past them, and saw down to my true self. He found me beautiful and engaging, and interesting. He would listen to me—me!" She twined her fingers through the fabric of her dress. "And he promised so many things, that we would be happy together, that we could grow old here. And when we did come here, I thought it would all come true." She looked up at me, tears glimmering in the soft light of the lamps.

It felt wrong for me to be hearing this, seeing these tears, but I did not stop her.

"Then the first ships landed on these shores." She shuddered. I could picture her standing on the walls of Ilium, her small hand wrapped in Paris', watching as the black ships of the Argives filled the horizon. "Living here was punishment, but can you imagine what Menelaus and his brother would do to me if they had me back?" Another shiver rippled through her shoulders. "There is no way...."

She sobbed on my floor silently for a time.

The rage inside me died, and finally, I slipped down to kneel before her. I had known women like her before. They had come to my mother seeking safety, seeking protection or meaning they would never find in their former lives. Otrera had helped them, and Hippolyta had after her. I had not. I had let my mother's dream die with my sister.

Worse, I had killed them both, dream and flesh.

"Why are you here, Helen?" My voice sounded soft, even to myself.

Helen bit her lip. "I am here because I cannot leave this city," she said. "I am here because my love for Paris has doomed us all." She reached out with her pale white hands to clasp my dark, calloused ones. I almost recoiled, so unfamiliar with such a touch, but I forced myself to hold still. Her fingers were soft but strong. "Why are you here, Penthesilea? When you could take your warriors and flee?"

"Priam needs me," I blurted out. Helen did not respond. She just waited for me, expecting me to say more.

Why did I need to explain myself? Priam did need me. He needed me to avenge his son. I was the only person with the skill and history to kill Achilles. The thought of him brought back the image of Achilles in my leopard skin. I was avenging Hippolyta's death—no, Hector's! "I must bring honor to the house of Priam. I must avenge Hector." But now it was not Hector's body I saw dragging behind Achilles' chariot, but my own Hippolyta's, bleeding from her gut where I'd stabbed her.

Helen squeezed my hands. "Perhaps Priam does not need you. Perhaps you need Priam."

Reluctantly, I tugged my hands back into my lap. "You should go," I said. I rose, then offered her my arm to help her up as well, which she took. She was so small and airy compared to me and my warriors, yet she did not seem weak.

When she reached the door, she turned back to face me once more. "You should go, too, Penthesilea," she said. "At least let your women go." Then she disappeared through the dark doorway, and I was, once again, alone.

The next day rose cool and sweet compared to the whole month before. Several clouds scudded across a bright sky, and breezes curling off the sea kept the walls of Ilium slightly chilled. I had risen at dawn to prepare for today's battle. My women had risen too, though I had not woken them and made their own preparations at my side. They were loyal to me and would fight for Priam as long as I asked them too. Together, we checked our weapons and harnessed our horses. The Argives and our allies traditionally did not ride but drove their cumbersome chariots to battle. Either that or they trudged on foot. We had learned long ago that horseback offered you more maneuverability and swiftness. Our steeds were smaller and sleeker than the giants who pulled the chariots. I patted mine, trusty Zephyr, on his cream-colored cheek. He snuffled happily into my palm. His calm extended to me, and I found myself soothed by his presence as always. We had ridden into a fight many times, and I had trained him myself from youth. Today we would ride against the Argives.

We had been given a stable far from where the chariot horses were kept. Though Priam treated us as allies, most of Ilium found women warriors distasteful and exotic — but not too distasteful that they wouldn't rely on us to save them.

My women seemed to share my thoughts. "All these men," laughed Antibrote, one of our number, "and they need a softer hand to win their war."

I laughed, we all laughed, but my hands were calloused and no softer than any man's. That's what men said about us, about women, that we were soft, gentle, delicate. I ran my fingers over the fletching of my arrows. I was not delicate. I had killed. Many times.

My sister's blood came to me, rising over the legs of my horse, threatening to drown me and Zephyr in an ocean of red gore. Hot blood, fresh from deep within her belly. It splashed against me, staining my hands. I blinked. There was no blood. The paving stones at my feet were dry and scattered with sand.

A horn sounded from the gates. The Argives were ready to make war on Ilium.

My women and I joined the warriors of Ilium at the gates in a blur of dust and horses and sweat. The white sun crept overhead as the Skaian Gates again swung open and illuminated the sands before us.

A scream erupted among the men, and their chariots rolled like tidal waves from the city. On the other side of the killing field, the Argives massed, armor gleaming, weapons drawn, horses nickering in anticipation. As soon as they saw us, they roared forward. It felt like seconds, and then the arrows began flying from one line to the other. Men cried out—some in triumph when their arrows thudded into the enemy, some in pain and terror as the darts struck them. Dust flew up in great clouds.

At the back of the line, I held my women steady. I scoffed. Chariots rumbled and disgorged men who pulled out swords and ran, screaming, at one another. Chariot fighting was so indelicate. So barbaric. But here, among these men, we were the barbarians. I adjusted my leopard-skin cloak and spurred on Zephyr. I would proudly be a barbarian if this were the only alternative.

My bow appeared in my hand, and I squeezed my knees tightly over Zephyr's girth. I aimed my first arrow towards the exposed thigh of an approaching Argive. A dark beard spilled from below his helmet, and his flesh was browned from the sun. The arrow flashed from my bow, sinking deep into his thick muscle, the fletching visible right against his skin now. His cry of anguish joined the regular sounds of the battlefield. I turned from him and sent another arrow into the slender neck of a man probably half my age. Blood spurted wildly and sprayed those nearby him.

At our feet and hooves, the bright sand turned to a churning, bloody mess. My women flew at my flanks. They, too, sent their arrows into the fray, always finding a home in some unfortunate man's chest or armpit or neck. Blood and screams doused us. Zephyr's strong hooves beat the ground, and any unlucky man who had fallen, as yet undead. But their bones broke and snapped under his and other hooves. They screamed. Their deaths would not be far off. I wheeled Zephyr to scan the field again. I could imagine daimones hanging over us all, waiting to slurp up souls and inciting more rage and violence in the fighters.

I tightened my knees around Zephyr and clenched my jaw. Another arrow found itself in a man's gut. He gurgled and fell to the sun-bright sands. I let loose another, this one to an old man, well past his prime. He fell without a sound. I was the avenging spirit here. Calm. Peaceful. Doling out death to those undeserving Argives. I was not wild like some of the men. My face was a frigid mask.

I would find no pleasure in killing, no pleasure in combat as I once had.

Not until I slew Achilles.

Achilles and his beetle-armed Myrmidons had not joined the fighting. Cowards.

So I envisioned each Argive man as an avatar of Achilles, one whom I slew with relish and satisfaction — but never glee. The only death that would please me was that of Achilles. Then I would drag his corpse after me like he did with Hector's.

Argive men fell all around me, some dead immediately, others bleeding to death on the sands. They would come around soon enough. They would die as their comrades did. Out of arrows, I took up a spear from some corpse and pierced the leather chest plate of a stately warrior. He dropped from his chariot. His driver gasped and tried to turn, but my sword found him too, and soon their horses rode onwards, free of the chaos of the battle. Zephyr whinnied sanctimoniously beneath me. He seemed to regard these horses as cowards as I regarded all the Argives. I laughed, the sound echoing about the field. I did not care what these men thought of me, ally or foe. Find me mad! That problem belonged to them. I was the right hand of Priam, slaying these Argive beasts for him. These multiples of Achilles would die, each and every one.

Then my women were around me, reining in me and Zephyr. They spoke to me, but their words rang against my ears silently. But I understood. For one of the few times in the whole length of this war, the Argives fled. The men of Ilium rejoiced and cheered.

"We must give chase!" I cried, trying to whip them into rallying behind me. "Come, let us bring this war to their threshold, as they have done to you!" I brandished my sword overhead like a beacon.

Some of the men turned to go with me, their eyes blazing with thoughts of revenge. But their generals shook their bearded heads dourly. "We must be patient." "We must not let them outsmart us."

Outsmart! A city under siege for ten whole years had already been outsmarted! I began to protest, but my women silenced me. Their hands and subtle head-shakes did more than these foolish arguments of Ilium.

As one, the host of Ilium turned back to the Skaian Gates. I turned my sweat-stained face to the sky and saw the sun had shifted significantly overhead. The fighting had lasted for some hours, I supposed, based on that and also on my tired, aching muscles and the amount of blood soaking Zephyr's flanks and my legs. The Argives must have been just as sore and beaten as us, but more so since they had retreated.

All the more reason to turn and finish them! I yanked Zephyr around and faced the enemy camp once more and saw smoke rising from beyond their pathetic ring wall of stakes. I could hear raised voices from the other side of the wall. Perhaps they were arguing there, as I had here, arguing to continue the fight, to lay down arms only when death claimed us all. My words, my voice, my argument, on the other side of those hateful stakes, beyond their pathetic trench. Someone there, I thought, was brave. Someone there had the gut and sense to keep on fighting. Keep on fighting until there was nothing left.

A heady wind swept in off the sea, jerking the crest of my helmet and waking me from my reverie. The others were nearing the gates at Ilium, but I still hesitated on the field between the great city and its invaders' camp. The ruckus within their bounds kept on. Something stirred in me, some great sense uncurling itself from slumber deep within my soul. Those men, those Argives, those monsters — they were not done.

"To me! Amazons, to me!" I cried, my voice carrying strongly over the sea wind. My women turned in their saddles and wordlessly came at my command. The men of Ilium turned languidly, not bothering to maneuver their chariots around to face our enemy.

"It's done, Penthesilea," called one of the generals, mayhaps some other son of Priam. "The battle is ours for today."

I spat in the sands. "No! They will attack again!" I dug my heels into Zephyr and sped back along the battlefield.

The men of Ilium scoffed, but some of the footsoldiers seemed to trust me and raced along with my women, trailing us like hunting hounds. Finally, the chariots lumbered about and slowly crept along behind us.

The gate at the enemy camp exploded then, disgorging chariot after chariot of dark-helmed men.

The Myrmidons. We had finally awakened Achilles and his Myrmidon warriors.

Chapter 6 - μικρὸς πόλεμος

THE LITTLE WAR

The wound on Hippolyta's forearm healed at last through no small effort by mother and the other healers on our island. For many weeks, she lay invalid in our own home, surrounded by women suddenly turned nursemaids, wrapped and unwrapped and wrapped again in as many bandages as they could keep clean. Balms and salves from the many native plants were crushed and daubed onto her arm.

All this happened at a distance. I, uninjured and bothersome, was relegated to my own corner of our home or to the rest of the village. Mother looked at me infrequently, her whole attention drawn by the danger of Lyta. Would the muscles heal? Would the wound sour? Would some brave soul attempt to sever her forearm with the hope of saving the rest of her from death? It was too much; I barely understood. And so I watched from outside the reaches of the caring women, puzzled by the activity.

The women were serious — no hand wringing or tears among the veritable troops of healers that entered our home. Not even mother seemed to cry, though her own daughter lay at the doorstep of Hades. Mother had taught me of death.

When the body died, Hermes, the psychopomp, drew the person's spirit into the land of the dead. Had Hermes come for Agathe's little son? Was his soul as mangled as his body by that beast? How lucky was Otrera that her daughters had not been killed like that.

But Hippolyta lived, and her arm healed, and soon she recovered the use of it. In the way of the very young, she seemed unscathed by the whole event, laughing soon after her recovery about the adventure of it all.

I, however, could still feel the cat's hot blood on my hands, feel the spray of arterial redness as it jetted upon my shaking body. I could still see Lyta's face contorted in terror when the cat pounced on her. I could still hear the wet thunks my blade made into the creature's body. The visions hovered in my mind at night. Dreams, they were, haunting dreams. Often I awoke frozen like a statue, fear coursing through my limbs until the sun sent glimmering rays through our windows and door.

And the cat had other ways of haunting my days. Soon after the event, when my mother was sure Lyta was not to leave our living world, Otrera pulled me aside and led me back into the forest. She stopped when we came upon the corpse of the cat. It no longer looked so threatening, lying there lifeless amongst the moss and leaves and dirt.

"This is your kill," she said, not facing me but keeping her eyes on the furred hulk. "Will you let it rot in the woods or bring honor to its life?"

I stared at the cat, digging my bare toes into the dirt. It felt somehow wrong for a small creature like myself to have bested this wild, beautiful, terrible thing. My face grew hot with shame and tears.

"I would honor it, Mother," I said in a quiet voice. "Like you honored Father."

Otrera took my hand and squeezed it between her calloused fingers. "That is good, child. That is good."

The big cat—called a leopard, I later learned—gave its pelt to me. Slowly and under the meticulous watch of my mother, I skinned the beast. Great tears gaped in the pelt where I had stabbed it, but with precise stitches, I did my best to sew closed the wounds, echoing the work done by the healers on Lyta's arm. When mother could not help me because she was looking after Lyta or doing some other work for our village, I worked with extra care and as slowly as I could to make sure I didn't ruin the pelt with some greater tear or poor stitching. The work was slow even when mother was there to supervise, but eventually, I had the pelt cleaned and sewn up properly. The rest of the cat's body had already been whisked away. I did not care where, for I never wished to see it again. So much blood and muscle. How could something with that much muscle have no life?

When complete, the leopard's pelt could cover me like a burial shroud—much too large for me to wear. Mother grinned at me when she saw me doddering around, blind under the spotted skin.

"Some day, Pen," she laughed, "you will grow into that pelt."

I, of course, did not believe her. This pelt would make a man look small. I would need to grow to be very tall.

Hippolyta, once recovered, joined me again in our childish games around the village. But we and the other girls rarely strayed as far into the forest as we had in the past. Though assured no more big cats lurked among the trees and brambles, we never felt fully sure of that. For we had never known the first cat was there.

Lyta's wound left her with a wicked scar, thick white snakes of skin that twined all the way around her forearm. But she and I grew so used to it after a time that I scarcely noticed the mark. We joked, ran, and played queen in the scrubby dirt between our village homes and knew peace and ease. Only the nightly reminder of the leopard, performed by the pelt Mother had hung on the wall above my bed, pushed any fear into my mind.

Peace came easy in our village, and more and more women joined mother. Apparently, word of our community spread throughout the world elsewhere, a world I had never known, for more women, and even some men, dregs of society, old, injured heroes and servants, orphans with no one to raise them—mostly it was women who found us a haven in the world of men beyond. For those without skills, mother taught them how to live and thrive on the island. She shared her knowledge of the world, which to a child, seemed more extensive than anything I knew or could ever hope to know. But even with the peaceful life we all lived, Otrera refused to leave us unguarded. Though mere women, she trained the younger, fitter ones in simple arms in case some new menace might threaten our peace. We remembered the cat that had killed Agathe's babe.

And there were worse things than cats in the world.

The next attack on our quietude came not from cats but from

drunken, stupid men.

As our community grew and flourished, men from the outer world licked their lips at our imagined treasures and girded their arms to take by force what was ours. The first of these was a small group that banked on our western shores. They came several days before another tragedy befell our people. Mother allowed the men into the village but asked they keep to themselves and promise not to harm any of the women there. And they did, mostly, drinking their wine and singing raucously in their own little encampment just outside ours.

In the first few years after the sad death of Agathe's infant, all our mothers were on edge, afraid that a creature like the leopard, or something more destructive, might threaten our bucolic existence. So they began to train us all not only in hunting but the wielding of arms. I, who had drooled over the weapons of my father, prayed to learn the way of his bronze sword. But mother did not think that a good place to start, and so the youngest of us were first taught more skilled work with spears and accuracy with bow and arrow. I grew proficient at both, rivaled only by my sister for better aim and strength. The other girls struggled a little, and Lyta smirked at them that we had the blood of the War God in our veins, so of course, we were superior. I did not argue, nor did the other children, but privately, I found the first rift between my thoughts and those of my sister. I suppose I believed in the existence of the gods—surely our Moon Goddess was real— but I doubted a god had sired us. That was too personal, too close, too mortal a job for a god. But how could I argue with my dearest Lyta? And so I kept my opinion to myself. Even mother encouraged her, so I felt I had no place to argue.

When the current crop of children was old enough, Otrera and the mothers assigned us scuffling matches. We wrestled and brawled, and those others watched the fighters. So we learned not only particular, prescribed techniques but also the way to win any fight, regardless of style. Black eyes and bruises and scratches and cuts were frequent visitors to our home. Each night, Mother would nurse our wounds, but I believed myself to be growing all the stronger for the melees.

There seemed to be a never ending supply of young women finding their way to our island. One, a girl not much older than myself or Hippolyta, appeared one day, her belly swollen large with child. My mother shook her head but accepted the girl into the village, letting her stay in a home nearby to ours, a home full of young mothers and their children. There was no assigned midwife in the village, but most of the women understood the subtleties of childbirth and rearing, so the house this girl moved into was the safest place for her. She rested most of her days. The strain of carrying a babe took quite a toll on her.

This was the first pregnancy I had experienced up close and with more than a child's mind. Otrera had explained that Hippolyta and I were nearing the age when we could, ourselves, become mothers, but I still had little understanding of the process. After all, with so few men in our community, and most of them past the age of siring children, the women who found themselves pregnant began the process elsewhere and only came to our island to birth the children. And so, when I wasn't scuffling or practicing archery in the forest, I stared through the wide windows of the women's hut and watched the young girl coo and moan over her own pain. I didn't feel particularly excited by her pregnancy—as in, I felt no urge or desire to become pregnant myself — but part of me held such curiosity for her condition that I could not help but watch. She seemed very much in pain. My own skin crawled at the thought of it.

Once, I mentioned to Hippolyta that I felt peculiar about the girl's condition, that it made me feel vaguely uncomfortable. Of course, Lyta's opinions were her own, and here I felt another tug of the catalyst that would sever our twin-like attitudes. Inseparable, we had been, up until this point, always alike in our thoughts and actions. But that would not last.

"I think I should like a baby," said Lyta, "someday."

I bit my lip. "I don't think I want to. Look how much pain there is to it. And then you have to raise the child."

Hippolyta laughed. "Yes, but isn't that the fun part?"

I shrugged. Perhaps I was too young to have an opinion on the matter. Perhaps my life would change these views. Privately, I felt that unlikely, but who was I to argue with my daring, charming sister?

Lyta occasionally sang little songs she'd made up about having a baby, but she mostly kept to herself on the matter, possibly to placate me. I grew edgier as the other woman's time grew near. At every ache, the young mother felt, I quivered. Every time she lay down, too tired to do anything, I shuddered. I felt an eerie discomfort any time I thought about her. I could not explain. Most other girls, including my Hippolyta, professed joy at the prospect of motherhood. But my body seemed to rebel, wanting nothing to do with such matters. I suppose I could have talked to Otrera about it, but she had birthed her own daughters and clearly didn't share my disquiet. Thus began my othering, whether I realized it or not.

The woman's baby came one morning, early or late, I never knew. But the birthing was not easy, that much I understood. Otrera and some of the other, more experienced women attended her in her bedchamber. Lyta and I were commanded not to enter unless Mother called for us specifically. The whole of the village gathered outside the small house to see the result of the birth and to hear the wails and moans of the mother. I vaguely recalled hearing Agathe give birth to her unfortunate baby before its untimely end, but these cries of pain seemed altogether too alarming and too frequent, even to an untrained ear. The men gathered from their camp as well, waiting at the outskirts of the group to see the result. They had been with us only a few weeks, but they understood the gravity of childbirth.

Hippolyta wrapped her arm around mine and squeezed. We were nervous. The whole town vibrated with an apprehensive edge. So far, mother had not requested us to aid her. I whispered a silent prayer to the Moon Goddess. The bedside of a birthing mother was the last place I wanted to be.

"Do you think it will be a boy or a girl?" asked Lyta. Her voice was light, but I, who knew her so well, could tell she was feeling jittery.

I played along, trying on the facade of calm as she did. "I hope it's a girl. That way, she can name her after our mother, and then we'll have a big Otrera running after a little one."

Lyta laughed a little, but the tension was not so easily broken.

The young mother screamed a sound that seemed wrenched from her body by an evil spirit. The scream echoed throughout the village. Then silence.

Finally, Otrera and the other helper women emerged, their faces drawn and haggard, dresses drenched in sweat and blood. Mother carried a small bundle, also bloody.

"The child," asked one woman, "is it all right?"

Otrera's head sank down to her breast, and she stared at the small figure in her hands. The beats of silence before she spoke seemed endless. Finally, she said, "The child lives. The mother lives. But I fear neither are long for this world."

Murmurs burbled through the crowd, the men at the back loudest of all. "If they live, surely you can keep them living." Others were more accusatory. "You women, with your witch magic — you can save them."

Otrera shook her head. "I'm afraid even the most gifted healers would have no recourse for these two." She drew back the top layer of cloth wrapping and revealed the child to the crowd. Stunned gasps, whimpers of horror, a physical shift of people back, away from the infant.

The child in Otrera's hands was red and ruddy from blood above and below the skin. He was unmistakably male, but the rest of his features twisted and curled in a cruel caricature of a human face. One eye bulged twice as large as the other. Even from here, I could tell he labored to breathe.

My whole body rebelled against watching, and I felt my hand go slack against Hippolyta's. Seeing the contorted figure in my mother's arms — the sight horrified me. I knew enough about babies to know this was not a healthy one.

From the back of the crowd, a man's voice lifted over the rest. "Looks like a healthy boy child!" slurred the drunken man. It was still early for one to be so drunk. "Give 'im a little milk, and 'is color'll settle down." The man pushed his way through the crowd until he was almost face to face with Otrera.

My mother shook her head sadly and covered the baby back up with his cloth, swaddling or winding cloth. I could not tell. "I'm sorry, sir," she said, "but this babe will not live out the night."

But the man, and increasingly his male comrades, would have none of it. They all pushed into the crowd and crowed about the ignorance of us women and the obvious health of the child. It was laughable. They were utterly wrong, and anyone could see it. Suddenly, they took hold of what they considered the obvious reason Otrera assumed the babe would die.

"You don't want him, do you?" cried one man. "You women just want some more girl-things around, and sod the boys!"

Hippolyta's hands tightened on my arm.

"What, do you kill all the boy-children here?" another man shouted.

Otrera handed the bundled babe to one of her midwife-aides, then raised her hands for quiet. "Please, you are guests on this island," she said, her voice hard as stone. "You have no right to question that which you do not understand."

"That's it, isn't it?" The men would not stop. "A whole island of witches, only women, and they kill any man they come across." Even though their presence upon the island refuted their argument, they all squawked in agreement. But they saw not their foolishness, only the proof that Otrera had doomed a male infant to die.

The violence erupted suddenly, like a tidal wave at one's back. The men who carried weapons drew bronze blades on the crowd. Those unarmed threw fists at those women closest to them. I saw one woman fall to the sword of a drunk, but the others scrambled away as best they could.

And then Otrera let out a cry. Part warcry, part whistle, part screech, only a harpy could have made such a sound. But it roused those women who were training us girls in the ways of combat, and they fought back against the men without hesitation, though their weapons were plough handles and spoons, brooms and sticks, rather than swords and daggers. Otrera herself led the fighting, and I saw her swirling through the crowd, rescuing women and beating back the attacking men like a storm. Hippolyta pulled me back until we were just under a hay cart, and so we watched from that short distance. We had no weapons, and though I felt much improved in our combat training, neither of us felt eager to jump into this bloody and destructive business. I felt my whole body frozen—I only moved because Lyta had tugged me away. Seeing the blood on the dirt and hearing the cries of pain from both sides of the skirmish chilled me to my belly. My limbs hung at my sides. I could not, would not move.

I could see the cat again, lunging towards Lyta. I heard her scream over the real screams of the wounded in the village. I felt the dagger in my hand and the blood of the cat running over my fingers again. But I was scared, so scared. Beside me, Lyta's eyes were round as a kylix.

The fight only lasted a few minutes, but to me, it extended into eternity. Quickly, Otrera brought the ringleader to his knees, holding a blade against his neck and quietly threatening his death unless his men relented. Hippolyta and I watched as our mother forced the men out of the town and back to the shore, where their boats awaited. She commanded in no uncertain terms that they leave and never return.

When we came back to the village, the newborn child had stopped breathing and died.

So there was nothing Otrera could have done to keep him living, just as she said. His mother had died too, so the midwife told us.

In the evening, after the sun set and the women returned from cleaning up the destruction to their own homes and hearths, Otrera put Lyta to bed. My sister fell asleep almost instantly, worn out from the wild events of the day. I remained awake, curled by the fireside and wrapped in the leopard pelt.

"We will have no more men here," said mother.

I nodded, though, at the time, I did not understand, not really what she meant.

"Things will be different for us," she added. "I fear you and your sister must train even harder. Our island may have become a target, or pariah, to those outside our shores."

I shook my head. "I don't want to fight, Mother," I admitted. I wrung the leopard pelt between my hands. "It scares me."

Otrera peered at me the way she had, reading more than was written on my face but down to my inner, secret self. "That is good, Pen. You should be scared. If you're not scared, the fighting can carry you away, carry you in the wrong direction."

This didn't make sense to me, and I must have shown my confusion.

"But being afraid doesn't need to make us unable to fight. Those of us who feel fear are the wiser fighters."

I nodded, but I don't think I understood, at least not that night in the glow of the hearth.

Chapter 7 - πόλεμος

THE WAR

The Argive attackers streamed from their camp, regular warriors trundling behind the leading Myrmidons. At the head of it all, leading the charge across the bloody field, was the prince of death himself, Achilles. His dark armor gleamed in the sunlight like onyx, brass and death, all mixed up and shining. Though armor wrapped around his entire form, I could still judge his body to be large and muscular, almost catlike in the graceful way he stood in his chariot.

I urged Zephyr forwards, my warrior women at my sides. All I heard were the thud of our horses' hooves against the hard-packed sand and the beat of my heart within my chest. There he was! My nemesis, the slayer of Hector, my next kill. I wished to the Moon Goddess that I had not spent all my arrows in the earlier fighting.

The men of Ilium, at last, realized what was happening and spurred their chariots and horses and footmen back out onto the battlefield. A chill ran through the air off the sea. Achilles had not fought anyone since Hector. And before that, he had refused to fight at all. I strained against the confines of my saddle, eager to be the one he met first on the field. Honor

meant nothing to me, nor did my legacy. In that moment, all I
desired was to avenge Hector.

The chariots of the dark-armored Myrmidons bounded
closer, their horses puffing and snarling like beasts of Hades.
Achilles let out a roar like a lion and cast his first spear. The
bronze tip whistled through the air and tore into the breast of
Evandre's horse in a mess of mangled ligaments and blood.
The steed squealed in its death throes, then toppled to the
sand. I spared a glance for Evandre, for I feared her leg might
be crushed under the creature's body, but she sprang aside in
the last moment, agile as all of the Amazons. She grabbed up
her javelin and continued to charge towards the Myrmidons.

The rest of us raced onwards towards the black-armed
enemy. The Myrmidon chariots fanned out into a wall as wide
as the battlefield. I kicked my heels into Zephyr, urging him
to meet Achilles. But somehow, just as the lines of Myrmidons
and the line of Amazons clashed, Achilles dropped back, and
I found myself facing some other nameless Argive warrior.
Snarling with rage, I launched a spear at the men and saw
it rip first through the breastplate of the chariot-driver, then
out through his back and into the gut of the weapons-dealer.
Together, they toppled off the back of the cart and onto the
ground.

I was already drawing my bow and wheeling Zephyr
around with my knees, sending arrows into the nearby
chariots. A man or two fell, but some gritted their teeth at
the wounds and kept on fighting. Gods, but these Myrmidons
were tough!

Where was Achilles? Zephyr and I cantered up and
down the battlefield, cheering on my Amazons and felling
any Argive who got too close. My blood burned hot in my

veins. Where had that beast gone, though, my prey, wretched Achilles? Everywhere I turned, his chariot was just riding out of my reach. Whenever I looked up from some petty sword-clash, he was always staring at me from the other end of the killing field. His eyes burned from either side of his helmet's nose guard, glowing like red coals, hot with killing fire. But I could never reach him. There were always too many warriors between us, too many paces to throw a spear or fire an arrow.

Argives besides the Myrmidons had joined the fight as well, and the soldiers of Ilium had rallied and banded together behind the Amazons, clashing again and again with those besieging their city. Such ferocity exploded from the defenders, as it only can from those losing a desperate fight. Many men died on both sides. But no women. All my Amazons, clever and nimble enough in their saddles, managed to dodge the Argive weapons, all the while dealing death and mayhem wherever they rode.

The presence of Achilles and his Myrmidon warriors had energized the Argives into a frenzy. For a few moments, I thought this battle might end, if not define, the war, but then the sides were dropping back, letting each other breathe for a moment. Or longer. Somehow, a truce was called for the evening, and chariots and riders and hoplites turned back to their respective camps. The fighting was over. No side had been a clear victor.

And I had not killed Achilles. He still lived. I thought my heart might beat out of my chest. Evandre, covered in blood and limping beside me, had to take Zephyr's reins and lead me back into the city. She saw the look in my eyes. She knew I might turn at any moment and launch my own charge on Achilles. The other Amazons gathered their horses around me, and together, we filed towards Ilium.

Seething, we passed the Skaian Gates and re-entered the city. People lined the walls and the main boulevards, standing as if to cheer on conquering heroes, but they remained silent. All across the breadth of Ilium, it seemed as though its citizens were holding their breath, afraid any exhalation might awaken some new onslaught from the Argives. Armor and weaponry, and gear clanked and rumbled as we flew back to the stables, but no one spoke. Even the banter among fighters was curtailed. I trembled with barely contained rage. Blood and gore coated my sword, but it was not the blood of Achilles.

Priam stood in the center of the large yard encircled by stables. I sent Zephyr straight past him, ignoring the wrinkled form of the king. Around him, his robes were rumpled. He stood and watched as all the warriors dismounted and led their horses to the charge of stable hands. I threw down my helmet and wiped the sweat from my brow as Zephyr's saddle and bridle were removed. The king hove closer to me and my women, but none would meet his eye except me. I fixed him with a glare so harsh and glowering that, though he was King of Ilium, he closed his eyes and bowed his head.

That was the power of Achilles. He had crushed the spirit of this regal man.

I barely remembered parting with my women, but eventually, as purpling dusk settled over the city, I found myself atop the wall above the Skaian Gates. Below, the great gates once again creaked open and disgorged the daily regiments of corpse-handlers. They would collect the dead and any useful weapons still on the field. Then the Argives would do the same with their fallen comrades. I stared down at them, cloaked in my own unspent anger. Why was Achilles not one of those fallen few? Why did the gods let him walk the earth still, after what he had done to Hector?

But then, why did they allow me my life after I killed sweet Hippolyta?

I found myself agreeing less and less with the decisions of the gods.

Before me, the killing field grayed as the sun descended, leaving the pick-up men to finish their work without the sun's aid. Their work was hard but not dangerous, for no one would break the nightly peace, despite the high tensions with the Argives. Some standards still had to be met, even in war. I shivered into my leopard skin. That was why Achilles' actions were so monstrous. I could accept killing — we all could. But no one could stand the sickening treatment of Hector's corpse.

A figure among the men near the bodies stole my attention. Unlike the flittering of the others, this man stood upright and stared across the sea of corpses to the Argive camp. I narrowed my gaze at him, for something about his bearing seemed altogether familiar. From this far, I could see little beyond a hoary head and stooped shoulders. It was an old man, then.

An old, stooped man intent on the enemy camp.

A man with little left in his heart to lose.

"Priam," I hissed. My own voice was less than a whisper, half of a breath, but it seemed as though the old man knew I had recognized him, and he turned to stare up at me. The sun had almost completely set, so there was barely any light, and he wore none of the usual trappings of his kingship, but that was Priam, feet planted in the sand and blood where I had slaughtered a great number of Argives.

He turned away after only a moment, and I pressed forwards, digging my hands against the rough stone of the battlements. The King of Ilium loitered among the dead! And the corpse-minders didn't even notice. My mind spun at the oddness of it, and I feared he had some dire mischief on his mind. Ilium could not survive without its king. It was barely surviving now.

I thundered down the steps that led down from the wall. A handful of guards occupied the walls, maintaining a constant but needless watch on the Argive camp, but they mostly ignored the crazed figure flying past them. I ignored them as well and brushed past their armored forms without a glance or word. I had to get to Priam. I had to stop him, whatever he was planning. Perhaps he had succumbed to the ultimate madness, the final desperation of one who'd lost everything and wished for his own death to come. My heart beat fast as I dashed toward the Skaian Gates, open ajar to let the corpse-handlers through. A few men were passing through the gateway with their stinking bundles wrapped tightly upon low carts. I pushed past them and crisscrossed the trail of similar men that wound between battlefield and city. At the edge of the field, too far from me and too near the enemy camp, the narrow figure of King Priam strode, a small stretcher bundled with small sacks dragging behind him in the sand.

King Priam made his way to the Argive camp.

Chapter 8 - μάθηση

LEARNING

Otrera refused to invite men to our island after the fight. The men who had come there previously, old grandfathers or lame sons, were not forced to go but asked politely to leave and not return. The fury of Otrera was something none of us had seen before and a wrath none of us wished to incur. Even Hippolyta, wild and free-spirited as she was, shrank back when mother spun through with her orders and her new commands.

The biggest change in our lives then was the weapons training. Since we had no men to rely on — nor could we have realistically relied upon the guardianship of a handful of ancient ancestors — Otrera commenced the full-scale training of women in arms of war. She did not let us use the arms and weapons gifted us by our father yet, but we were given fresh spears and a bow each and told to fashion our own arrows for killing men and not hunting in the underbrush. The transition went smoothly. We became accustomed to following the various trails about our island, scanning the trees and grasses with increasingly trained eyes to spot signs of male incursion. It was not a question of would the men return but when.

One night, all of us sweating from bouts of spear-fight training, Otrera called us close to the hearth in our small home.

"My daughters," she said and smiled. Both Lyta and I curled our legs under ourselves and settled down on the woven rug before the hearth. We had grown much over the last winter, and Mother barely needed to look down at us any longer. "My daughters, there is much for me to teach you."

Hippolyta laughed in that sparkly, dreamy way of hers. "Oh, Mother, I doubt there is time enough in the night, or the year, for all the things we have to learn from you."

Otrera chortled at that, and I smiled though I waited more patiently for our mother to explain herself.

"There is talk among us of sending some of the daughters away," began Mother. "The girls would be taught the ways of the world in a larger city and learn to fight and defend themselves by the greatest warriors." She paused and looked at both of us. "The purpose behind this fosterage would be to make our daughters greater warriors — greater than we could hope to train here."

"But you are the greatest warrior, Mother!" exclaimed Lyta. "Why send girls to train with someone else?"

Mother composed her thoughts to answer when I cut in, "Are you sending us, too?"

Silence reigned, not even a breath, besides the crickle crackle of the gentle fire. Then, Mother bowed her head. I had never seen such obeisance in her before. There was something strange about it. It made me edgy, but we did not argue with her.

"Yes, my dears," she said at last. "I need you to learn to be strong warriors. And I know of a king who has the best training in all these lands. His name is King Priam, and he rules a city called Ilium. I have already sent word to him that you will be traveling there, along with some of the other girls from our island, to learn the ways of the weapons of man."

I did not argue, nor did Hippolyta. How could we? Our beloved mother, whom we trusted in all things, had made a decision. We were expected to obey her. And it was not so hard a thing to obey someone whom we both adored. It was hard to think of leaving the island, though, our homes for all the time we could recall. I realized I didn't even know if we'd been born here or not, but truthfully, it did not matter because this island was our home.

And so we spent our time waiting for the men of Priam to come and take us all away. For my part, I filled my time with training and exercise. I had a vague notion that women were not usually cast as fighters and decided that I wanted there to be no doubt in this Priam's mind that I could wield a blade as well as any boy my age could. A few of the other girls joined me in racing around the sandy shores, the thick, sucking sand an extra difficulty in our training regimens. We were all becoming older together, but not so old that we could not laugh and jest and joke with one another still.

Hippolyta began to drift from us, joining our sparring matches occasionally but mostly spending time on her own in the woods far from the village. I did not like her growing distance from us and especially from me. I felt like a spool of thread, unwinding slowly. The farther she went and the more time we spent apart. Did Lyta not love me? Why was she not at my side, leading the other girls through our practices? Mother, preoccupied with fortifying the island and forging plans for our futures, hardly noticed Lyta's remoteness. I tried to mention it to her, but she was too busy to listen to her half-grown daughter's laments.

And so one day, after weeks of such growing separation, I, too, left the other girls to their own work and slunk into the woods. High overhead, the sun shone brightly, but the tree branches latticed themselves across the sky and kept most of the harshness from my eyes. With the care of a burgeoning hunter, I stalked down the path that Lyta had taken that morning. The reason I'd chosen that particular day to follow her was what she had carried with her when she left—a small satchel tucked under one arm. Why, I wondered, would she need such a thing out here? What was she doing off in the forest? I kept to the shadows as much as I could, which wasn't hard and soon found myself halfway across the island, still pursuing my errant sister.

Then, a sound reached my ears.

A giggle. Then a throaty, hearty laugh.

One belonged to my sister. The other—I did not recognize.

I crouched in the brush, suddenly feeling very out of place. I had never felt out of place on the island before, not when we found the man's corpse, not when the leopard attacked. But the hushed words and the escaping mirth from Hippolyta and her mysterious someone caused me to shrink in my sandals. I was not supposed to be here. I was not meant to hear or see any of this.

Lyta was hiding something—no, someone—from me.

I crawled forwards and peered through the fronds of a dense fern. There were two figures reclining in the grass.

Lyta was hiding a man from me.

I supposed I had never seen a naked man before, or not

one this young and vigorous. Though young, younger than the old grandfathers who'd lived in our village as of late, this man was still older than Hippolyta and me by a good many years. His hair was tousled golden-brown and fell around his thick, muscular shoulders. The shoulders and the rest of him glowed like a flame, ruddy and gilded from the sun. He threw back his head and laughed at something humorous Lyta had whispered in his ear. My sister was entwined between well-muscled legs, with her fingers playing lightly against his golden flesh. The intimacy, the connection between them, almost sent me flying back towards home. But I knew that if I got up and ran away, they would certainly notice me. And I still needed to understand what was happening, understand why Lyta had kept this strange man from me and Otrera.

The sack Hippolyta had carried was sprawled open at their sides. In it were bits of food and a cask of wine. And a dagger in its sheath. I could tell it was not one of the daggers from our father, and I sighed with relief. At least those items, my inheritance, was safe. For some reason, in this odd interval, that notion comforted me.

Lyta reached out a hand and coyly caressed the man's cheek. Rumbling like an animal, he grabbed her wrist. She laughed, he growled some more, and they crashed into each other with passion. I watched for only a moment, then turned away, tears filling my eyes for no reason at all.

I scurried away as quickly as I could, though they had no concern for anything but each other. As I raced back home, the unshed tears now dripped down my face, mixing with the dirt and dust I kicked up. I felt too young but trapped in a body that didn't understand the desires and wants of others, too stupid to know what men and women did together, and too dispassionate to crave what came naturally to others.

I held my tongue about the man, even when Lyta returned home that night glowing like a firebrand and smiling like a loon. Maybe Otrera assumed we had spent the day together. I did not know. I turned aside from them as we dined in silence, choking on the unspoken thoughts filling my mind. A man! And here on the island, after Mother forbade it. Oh, Lyta, what game are you playing?

I could see shortly that it was no game. For she stole nothing more than handfuls of food from our home over the course of the next few days. I knew the man must still be hiding himself in our woods, though I refused to go again lest I catch sight of them taking their pleasures together. The idea of it nauseated me. I knew it was a natural act, that much I knew, not the mechanics really, but the human need for it. But I didn't feel the desire, the ache to belong to someone else. I wanted nothing. I desired nothing. For some reason, most of my disgust faced inwards rather than at Hippolyta. She was the normal one, I thought. And I was someone wrong or broken for not feeling as she did.

It hurt, and I turned away from the other girls. At last, Otrera seemed to notice something was wrong now that I was sullen and dour and keeping to myself.

"What is wrong, my little warrior?" she asked. "Why are you so distant from us?"

I shrugged. What could I say that wouldn't betray Hippolyta or paint myself as a freak?

"Are you upset I am sending you to Ilium to train?" When I shook my head, she patted my hair down. "Whatever is wrong, Pen, trust that I love you. You're my strong girl. My warrior girl."

"If I'm a warrior, what is Lyta?" I asked. I was starting to see differences between me and my sister, but I couldn't understand them or why they existed in the first place. Weren't we all just people? Mortals? And so I asked my mother to know what she thought of Hippolyta.

Mother smiled and twisted dark strands of my hair around her finger. "Lyta is strong as any warrior, too. But she is a dreamer, a queen of dreams." She released the curl, which sprung upwards. "And so I have a dreamer queen and a warrior queen. Neither one is bad, Pen. Don't look upset."

I wasn't upset, not as I understood it. I was just confused. I fidgeted where I sat and suddenly realized I was almost as tall as Otrera, if not the same height. When had I grown? When had Hippolyta and I grown from girls into women? That idea terrified me. I did not feel ready to be my own person, to fight, to love, to dive into the world on my own—not yet, not yet. Not yet.

Otrera must have read the feelings struggling their way across my face and, whether she understood exactly their cause or not, tucked me into her arms like she had done when I was little and hummed away my pain. Sleep came a little easier after that, but my dreams were still filled with confusion and sorrow.

Several more days went by before I realized Hippolyta's man was a problem. I had still practiced some with the other girls, training as my mother desired, but one day in the afternoon, I was filled with the desire to look upon my father's weaponry and armor. My heart swelled at the thought of seeing his glorious helmet, of taking his bronze sword into my hand.

But when I opened the woven trunk wherein Mother had stored the relics, I found none. The helmet, the cuffs, the belt, the blade — all gone.

Mother was not there, and I was glad, for I knew where the items had gone. Or who had taken them. And why.

I raced out of the house and into the forest. My bare feet flew almost silently across the forest floor, fleet as a deer. Hippolyta's presence tugged at me like a lodestone, and though I did not know exactly where on the island she might be cavorting with her lover, my feet found her soon enough. They were stretched out beside each other on a beach on the far side of the island. I burst from the treeline onto their sands and saw the detritus of my father's legacy strewn around them.

"Pen!" cried Lyta, bouncing up when she saw me. She tugged her chiton closer around her body. The man with her rose slowly, so much like the leopard moved, his eyes never leaving my face.

"What are you doing, Lyta?" I shouted. No tears formed in my eyes, but I felt my face burn red. "Are you stealing for him? Did he ask you for our father's things?"

Lyta reached one hand to me and another to her lover, meant to calm one or both of us. It did not work.

"I'm not stealing anything, Pen," Lyta tried to explain. "I just wanted to show him." She smiled at me. "Don't be upset with me. Here, let me introduce you. This is my friend. His name is Heracles."

The young man straightened himself up to his full height, which was taller than both Hippolyta and myself. He inclined his head wearily. "I take it this is your sister, then?" he asked of Lyta.

I didn't wait for an introduction or response of my own. "Why do you want to see our father's arms? Are there more men here? Are you alone?"

My sister rolled her eyes. "He's alone, Pen. It's just him. He arrived a few weeks ago. But you know I couldn't tell Mother about him, not after she just forbade men from the island."

Heracles' brow furrowed. "I was just stopping here. I don't want any trouble from you or your man-hating kind."

Hippolyta turned to him in shock, losing grip a little on her dress as she did. More of her golden skin slipped into the sunlight. "'Man-hating?' We don't hate men here. Wherever did you get that idea?"

But Heracles was also reaching for his own belt to clasp around his waist. A sword hung from it. "We've all heard of your island of women. All the girl-lovers and moon-worshippers. The killing of any man who sets foot here, even infants. I see now it's true." He shook his head to Lyta, but his attention still sulked around me. "I should leave. A man does belong here."

Hippolyta tried to argue, but Heracles would have none of it. I watched as he dragged a small boat out from under the brush and pushed it through the sands to the beach. He dumped his few belongings into the bottom of the round craft and accepted only a tankard of water from my sister before he made to set sea. After a few minutes of working in silence, Lyta accepted that he was leaving and helped him push the little craft out towards the sun-glittering waters.

I watched it all like a hidden observer, like a bird on a

branch, not the cause of the disruption itself. I felt angry—at myself for exploding at a stranger, at Lyta for lying to us all, and at Heracles, whose eyes lingered greedily on the bronze weapons and armor that littered the beach. For a moment, I thought he might take Lyta with him, but she remained firmly planted with her feet in the sands.

"It was a pleasure, Hippolyta," he said, one foot swung over the bow of his boat, the other calf-deep in seawater. "Maybe I'll see you again someday."

Hippolyta looked upset, but no tears had yet stained her cheeks. "I shall miss you, Heracles."

He grinned. "I hope so."

"Wait!" Before he could climb aboard his little craft, Hippolyta raced back to the beach and grabbed up one of my father's items, the gleaming metal belt. "Here," she said, placing it in his hands and letting her fingers trace their way across his forearms the way I'd spied her do days ago. "To always remember."

I bit down my arguments at my sister, deciding it was better to wait until the interloper was gone. But this, I did not like. How had she the right to give away our father's things? Were they not also mine? And what of our mother?

Heracles leaned forward and kissed Lyta full on the mouth. I hated the intimacy of it and being forced to watch. "I don't think I could ever forget my beautiful sea queen." He ran his finger down the curve of her jawline before climbing into his boat with the belt clutched to his breast.

I wanted to shout my apologies to Hippolyta as I watched her stand at the edge of the sea while Heracles drifted further and further away. But when she turned around, I found her eyes clear and her face clean of any anger or resentment.

How she did not hate me, I could not understand. In fact, I could understand little of what had happened here.

"Lyta…." I began haltingly.

"Pen, please," she cut in. She walked up to me and took my hand in hers. "I know I shouldn't have let him stay so long. And I should have known I couldn't keep a secret from you." She smiled with a ruefulness I had never seen her express before. "All things have their time, and ours was just about over anyway." She tugged at my hand. "Come, let us go home."

Silently, almost peacefully, we gathered up the arms of our father and other items Lyta had brought here, brushing off the sand and fallen leaves. I felt an inner anguish at myself, at her, at our mother, at the man, at the other men who started the fight in the village, at the leopard, and even at the Moon Goddess. Bitterness soured the day as we trudged back home, my face dark and Lyta's bright with the memories of first love, laughter, and ardor.

Chapter 9 - πόλεμος

THE WAR

Cursing, I sped up, but I knew that he would reach the Argive camp before I could catch him. I passed the chariot wrecks and corpses of horses, yet the old king always stayed just so far in front of me. How was it that he, who could barely sit upon his throne without quivering and looking about to topple over, now strode into the camp of his enemies, head held high, shoulders thrown back?

I tugged my leopard skin about me, then shrugged. How could I, a woman armed like a man and wrapped in this unusual pelt, expect anonymity were I to enter the Argive camp? The thought hit me as ridiculous, and I spared a moment to scan the wreckage left behind. A ragged tract of fabric, dark in the ill-light, maybe black or brown or blue, shivered in the light breeze. A shattered chariot held down one of its corners. The blanket or cloak or saddle cloth gestured at me, and I knelt down to shift the wood and release the mantle. Once done, I pulled it about my body the way the sun wraps itself in harsh, thick clouds during a storm.

I stood to follow Priam and his mysterious stretcher. Perhaps he entered the enemy camp to relieve himself of life, to substitute his own death for all of ours. I hoped not. Priam was still Priam, king of Ilium, and I doubted his people would fare well without him. Who would rule after him? That idiot Paris? His decisions had already doomed them well enough. I shuddered to think of what more problems that one could foist upon Ilium. He had shown a great talent for it thus far.

Past the field of battle, Priam led me across the little stream that trickled into the bay, splitting the landscape between Ilium and Argive camp from north to south. The river had shrunk since last I'd seen it, but its waters felt cool to my weary feet as I trod from one bank to the other. Our path angled north once we crossed the little river, north to the camp of the enemy.

The walls of the Argive camp jutted from the earth in a weak mockery of Ilium's shining ones. I had not yet been this close to the camp, and I peered over the embankment and into the pit that surrounded the camp proper. The trench snaked around their camp, bristling with broken spears, bits of shipwreck, and anything that might injure a falling man or horse. Guards manned the entrance to the camp, but they looked anything but watchful. And why should they be? My comrades had crossed the gap only once, I'd heard tell, and recently, when great Hector led his men almost up to Agamemnon's sleeping tent. Only Hector could lead such an attack. No other man at Ilium was brave enough or confident or daring.

And now there was no Hector. I had done my best earlier that day but failed. Hector had been a better fighter than I. Once more, I scoffed at mother's claims that some god had fathered me. There was no more god's blood in my veins than in any beggar or thief on the street. But Hector had flown like the son of a god and had fought like one of the gods himself.

I lurked around the camp, seeing no sign of old Priam. Mayhaps he had straggled through the main gateway at the heels of the Argive's own corpse-men. I eyed the wooden walls, trying to make out as much as I could of their make in the darkness. Taller than a man, by nearly double, but only one or two layers of wood thick, the walls seemed to me more pretense than defense.

The enemy camp was vast, much larger than I had anticipated, having seen them from atop the walls of Ilium. It stretched on and on into the night, the glow of campfires and torches beyond the walls casting yellow light upwards to the stars. At last, I reached another gate. I reasoned that the main gate would be too obvious, but a lesser gate might be easier to penetrate. Apparently, the guards on either side of the makeshift gateway agreed—with my dark cloak, helmet, and height, I looked enough like the Argive warriors that they simply nodded me through. It would not be honorable to use this opportunity to slay Achilles and the Argive leaders, but I was sorely tempted as I slunk into the camp.

Tents hung from and pressed up against the sides of ships, long since beached and made decidedly un-seaworthy with big openings carved into the hulls and boards pried off and used elsewhere in the busy place. Narrow, crooked lanes led between the unplanned and scattered living spaces. I followed one dusty path towards the heart of the camp. Soldiers were everywhere, cooking over small fires, honing weapons, fixing armor, and chasing women and young boys through the sandy streets. Noise and the smell of sweat hit me in equal measure, and I wasn't sure which appalled me more.

The Argives were a lusty lot, and voices were raised in song all around the camp. Some even sparred with one another in friendly bouts, kicking up sand as they circled and pounced on one another. I shook my head. How could anyone still want to fight? Hadn't they been here for almost ten years? Was this war that slowly killed Ilium not enough? I was sick of everything, and I had only just arrived in this hellish place.

The curlicue roads twisted between beached ship and hut and tent, and I could make out no pattern to the layout. Perhaps the men were divided by clan, by town across the sea. Was there any rule to this community? I knew that Menelaus and his brother Agamemnon, kings of the west, had brought together this massive force and kept them together by some power of their own, but maintaining peace and law in a group so large — much greater a number than a small town or even an average sized city. There must be laws, must be guardians, must be punishment.

But so far, these men seemed lawless to the extreme, especially considering Achilles' desecration of Hector's corpse. Men like that were hardly men. Clearly, no laws governed warriors like him. Men like Achilles thought they were gods or part-god or some other nonsense. Despite my mother's claims about me and Hippolyta, I knew better. Achilles was just as much flesh and blood as any other man here. Judging from the smell, they all sweat and bled and pissed the same.

I rounded a harsh bend around a series of patched and stained tents. The smell of manure and livestock hit me. A large pen of goats and pigs stretched to my left, and I instantly thrust myself down any other pathway at random. The sand churned beneath the feet of the animals into a poisonous, malodorous melange that even my strong stomach refused to handle. My eyes stung as I rushed in the opposite direction, still trying to make my way towards the center of camp. I hoped from there I could find the quarters of Achilles and his men, where I assumed Priam had headed. As I ducked out of the way of a number of men strung out across the road, drunk as maenads and laughing boisterously at some joke one or other of them had made. Though it was dark, still I leaned my head down, hoping to conceal my features in the shadows of my helmet. No other women went armed like me and my women, and it would not be hard to guess my identity were I captured. But the Argives were drunk and idiotic and inattentive. They might be worthy fighters on the battlefield, but in camp or at home, they devolved into silly creatures, as most men did. Still, I wanted the attention of a wine-muddled Argive man as much as a pitched battle right now. I had to find Priam.

The king of Ilium walked unguarded and possibly unarmed in the camp of his enemies. Only I knew where he'd gone—probably Hecuba had spent many nights alone since this war started and hadn't even noticed her husband was missing. After all, he may have still had other wives besides Hecuba. Perhaps she thought of him visiting one of them. Although how any man could desire a woman—or a man—after seeing Hector's body so, that I would never understand.

Finally, the king! I caught sight of Priam ahead of me, laboring against the weight of the stretcher that dragged behind him. Try as he might, he could barely weave through the throngs of soldiers and hangers-on, and I saw him stumble and slip one knee onto the sand. I considered pushing aside a fat man leading a pig but shrank back. No, I thought, nothing to draw attention to myself.

Ahead, Priam moaned but managed to rise. Grabbing ahold of the ropes attached to the front of the stretcher, he heaved and continued on his way. I strode along behind him. With no reason to make myself more suspicious, I thought to blend in with the other warriors in the camp.

Priam staggered his way through the enemy camp, and I followed. Inexorable was his path. To what foreign king did he mean to barter? And would he barter riches or himself?

But I knew, deep within my darkened heart, exactly where he was headed. I knew without a doubt to whom he hoped to negotiate. For all the Argives and their riches, mostly stolen from the Troad coast and nearby islands, there was only one treasure worth anything to old King Priam.

The body of Hector.

Priam meant to entreat the monster, Achilles.

Priam meant to parley with the worst of our enemies.

I gasped, the feelings of hatred and rage stabbing me deep in the gut like a rusty blade. I had planned to protect Priam, to make sure he survived his journey into the heart of his enemies' camp, but against Achilles—even I could not promise to remain clear-headed. Already, the fog of war, the cloud of anger, began to build behind my eyes, tinting the world red and fiery. I clenched my fingers, only to find them already on the hilt of the dagger at my belt.

To kill Achilles.

That was why I had been brought to Ilium.

I would kill Achilles. Tonight.

Chapter 10 - πρώτα

THE FIRST

We arrived at Ilium just after dawn, us girls from our small island. Ships—boats, really, but we'd never seen anything quite so grand as the craft that came gliding across the sea to collect us—crawled across the narrow waters of the Hellespont and into the bay that squatted before the great walled city of Ilium. We, who had known no more than the airy walls of our island at the mouth of the river Thermodon, gaped at the sight. Ilium was a city. A god among cities. I could barely fathom anything larger, anything grander.

I and the other girls, there were twelve besides myself and Hippolyta, crowded the prows of the pair of ships. We were pointing and laughing and shouting across the sparkling waves to each other. The rising sun glinted off the sea, reflecting its light and our hopes back into our eyes and glinting against the creamy, white walls of Ilium.

The two ships nosed gently into the harbor, steered by expert hands towards the collection of other, beached and anchored watercraft along the bay's shore. The city itself sat a bit inland of the bay, surrounded by fields and vineyards and flocks of sheep and goats and people, oh, so many people.

I could see their small forms beetling all along the horizon. I drew in a deep breath. Here, laboring like ants within the vista of Ilium, were more people than I had ever seen than I had ever imagined. And we were still so far out! I grasped Hippolyta's hand and squeezed as I had done many times during our childhood. She squeezed back. We were both children again in the sight of this massive place.

"There are so many people," I breathed.

She nodded. "It almost seems unreal," she replied, just as quietly.

She was right. How could there be this many mortals outside the walls of Ilium? And what did that mean for the rest of the world? I felt suddenly small, smaller than the smallest mouse in the underbrush of Otrera's island of women. Thinking of my mother's silly title — "warrior queen." I was nothing of the sort, not when there was this mess of life, this abundance of humanity out here that I had never conceived of. I had thought Lyta and I were so big, so grand, so important. Now I could see there was just so much more.

Eventually, our ships reached the shoreline, and we clambered out, splashing a little in the waves and the sands as we regained our steadiness on land. Collecting ourselves and our meager supplies, we barely noticed as a large party of men came down to the beach to greet us.

It was Hippolyta who noted their presence first and whistled to us to attend. King Priam marched on his own robust, royal legs, trailed by colorful courtiers and an endless line of young men, all bearing a similarity of face to him that identified them as his own spawn. By the gods, the man had been busy! Squinting into the white sun's glare, I could barely count how many sons the man had brought down to greet us. Priam smiled at us from under palm fronds held by his servants.

"Welcome, daughters of Otrera and other girls of Themyscira," he intoned. His name for our island jarred like a thrown stone against my ears. I supposed our homeland had a name, just as Priam's did, but it was so rarely used by anyone but a stranger that I had almost forgotten it existed. Themyscira, little town on the island by the river called Thermodon. It was a bigger river than the one I saw now that fed into the bay just to the west of Ilium, but not by much. I wondered if these men thought us uncouth and barbarous, for we harked from no city with high walls or endless vineyards or dozens of servants. I straightened my back proudly, just in case they did.

Hippolyta and I stepped out before the line of other girls and bowed to the king. He looked on us appraisingly, not quite as one might inspect a piece of meat but something similar.

"We are humbled to accept your offer of fosterage, great king," said Hippolyta. She spoke her greetings proudly but with just enough courtesy to not sound rude. It was good she was our spokeswoman; I was not sure I could have managed such fealty to a stranger.

"Long ago," began King Priam, a smile curling his lips, "I had the pleasure of meeting your mother. A woman like no other. I see her daughters and their companions are just the same. It honors me to welcome you into my city and have you train arms beside my own sons."

One of the many similarly-faced boys snorted. Priam shot a look at the boy, who had bright hair like a flame and was my junior by at least several years.

Priam cleared his throat as if we hadn't heard the audacity and accusation in his son's snort and continued. "It is true that we do not train our own daughters to fight, for that is a man's job. However, the request of Queen Otrera holds certain sway here, and so we shall instruct you in all our ways."

Just like the name of our island, hearing mother referred to as "queen" shocked me. Luckily, we were bowing again, so I could hide the smile that quirked my mouth. When I rose, I found another son of Priam, this one about my age and dark of hair, staring at me. His eyes held none of the rudeness of his brother, but he seemed particularly intrigued, which set my skin crawling. I had no wish to draw the attention of any man, not even a son of a king. But, of course, I was an oddity — a girl who fought and who stood taller than most men — and I was bound to suffer under the eyes of others. The son of Priam noticed I had caught him staring and experimented with a grin that seemed both forced and genuine, as if he couldn't decide whether he was disgusted by us girl warriors or wanted to be the best of our friends. I ignored him, hoping to lose sight of him in the crowd of other princes as we began to follow Priam's entourage back into Ilium.

As ever, my luck refused to hold, and soon Hippolyta and I — leading the other twelve girls — were joined by the dark-eyed boy. Lyta smiled and greeted him while I disguised my rolling eyes by stretching my neck.

"They're calling you Amazons," said the boy. He was around my age or my Lyta's, but his voice was still settling into manliness. He blinked more than I thought a royal heir ought to.

"They can call us whatever they like," I retorted.

Lyta nudged my arm. "Pen! No need to be rude. Especially if it's a name mother herself has used." She smiled across me at the boy. "My name is Hippolyta, and this is Penthesilea, my sister and the grumpiest harpy this side of Phrygia."

The son of Priam laughed, an open sound that tried to force a smile from my face. "I'm Hector," he said. "I'm one of Priam's sons." His open, friendly face did its best to calm my earlier edginess. "I hear we're to train with you. I've never fought a girl before."

"I don't think there's much difference between fighting a girl and fighting some pimply boy," I said.

"Oh, there would be quite a few differences, I'd say," added Lyta bawdily.

Hector's tanned face turned bright red. "I only meant, uh, arms training and archery and the like. I never—"

This time I cut in to save the poor lad from paroxysm. "Don't worry, Hector, that is what I knew you meant. My sister is just trying to rile you up." I glared down at Hippolyta, who had not grown nearly as tall as I had. "We promised Mother not to start any trouble." I arched a brow.

Otrera might not have seen Heracles with Lyta or known specifically of his presence, but the tone had changed a bit at home before we left. Our mother had spent almost equal time instructing us in fighting and comportment among civilized people as she had the topic of all the lusty young men we were assumed to meet. While she never forbade us from laying with men, she counseled wisdom in such encounters, for where a man might fly untethered into the night, a young woman might find herself child-heavy and quite indisposed. I knew she meant to keep us safe and honest during our trials at Ilium—and I knew she and the other women had similarly advised our companion girls—but I also felt deeply that I would have no trouble keeping my word on the matter. I had seen a man and felt nothing, no desire, no pull, and I had seen women and felt the same. Surely, I would have no trouble with the handsome, carefree boys of Priam's household. But—and this I promised myself secretly—I would keep a keen watch on Hippolyta, lest she go looking for another dalliance like the one with Heracles that had lost us our father's belt.

But this Hector recovered from Hippolyta's teasing and focussed his attentions more on me than my sister as we trudged under the hot sun and across the sandy soil up to the city. He pointed out towers and buildings that rose from behind the impressive city walls, he named royal advisors and courtiers among the king's party, and he listed his many brothers and fellow princes who had joined Priam on the outing. None of the other boys showed much interest in us other than the occasional appraising glance or titter of laughter between two or three brothers. Hector alone seemed a friendly presence in Priam's sea of sons. I decided to be civil to him until he proved himself otherwise.

We entered the city through a massive gateway, which Hector called the Skaian Gate. The portal was so large I thought the entire island of us Amazons might be able to rise from the sea and float through the gate easily without jostling a handful of sand from the shorelines. Never had my wildest notions of the outer world prepared me for the utter largeness of Ilium. The curtain wall of the city and the gatehouse around the Skaian Gate was made up all of limestone blocks, again so very large. I had no idea how simple men might have arranged them in such great quantity and formed so strong a bastion. Inside, the walls impressed me all over again, as all the buildings lining the main road were also made of stone and brick. And I had gotten so used to the greens and browns of home, the yellow of flowers and the blue of the water and sky, that a limestone city shocked me to my soul.

As part of the parade following King Priam through the city, I and the other girls were privy to the bowing and general obsequiousness of the population. The honor they paid their king was so different from the friendly hails and greetings thrown to Otrera back home, though apparently, she was lauded as a queen just as Priam was king. Which made me and Hippolyta equal in standing to this Hector and his passel of brothers. I would have to remember that.

Deep into the city, we trekked until I thought my legs might give out before we entered the palace of Priam. Surrounded by its own lesser walls, Priam's home and seat of rulership rose above the rest of the city in a series of colorfully painted buildings. To see the white gleaming stone corrupted by so much red and blue and yellow paint irked me—but it was not my city. Probably these people would be just as offended by the simple, wood-walled homes of Themyscira.

I and the other Amazons were housed in our own barracks building with a staff of female servants. Otrera was not the only one concerned with the honor and parturition of the girls. That first night, Hippolyta gathered all the girls into a common room within the barracks and praised each of us for being so brave to have traveled all this way into the relative unknown. It was true that while fourteen of us had left the island to come to Ilium, there were quite a few other girls who had refused and stayed home. My sister called each girl by name—"Alkibie, Thermodosa, Polemusa, Derinoe,

Hippothoe, Derimachea, Bremuse, Klonie, Antandre, Harmothoe, Antibrote, and Evandre" — and handed each a word of commendation. I sat in the corner between Klonie and Polemusa. My heart swelled. I had not thought my sister capable of such a touching tribute, and I knew the other girls felt supremely honored by it. After we went off to our own bunks to sleep, I wondered at the great show of beneficence displayed by my dear Lyta. Truly, I thought, she had the makings of a good queen.

Our training began every morning at first light. The sun seemed always to hang right overhead in Ilium, finding any bare inch of skin on the body and burning it to a crisp in a matter of moments. How I wished for the trees and overhanging branches of our home! How I dreamt of the cool breezes and soft shadows of our island!

But I did not complain, and, to their credit, neither did any of the other girls. A doughty, middle-aged lord named Anchises — some cousin or other of Priam — took charge of our education and the education of the palace's youths, including his own rangy son Aeneas, the innumerable sons of Priam, and other royal relations of the right age and gender. Lord Anchises was all stringy muscle and parched skin, and after the few boxes on the ears, most everyone learned to obey his commands. When we were not casting spears or shooting arrows at targets, skirmishing with real, bladed swords, or learning to chop with the battleax, Anchises set us to running circles around the walls of Ilium.

"Keeps the blood up," he would say before sending the whole profusion of us on another lap or five. I learned quickly that the city of Ilium was very wide. On our runs, Hector would often join me. Whenever his eyes sparkled in my direction, I would sprint away, trying to outpace the highest heir among Priam's sons. Sometimes he would beat me, and sometimes I would beat him, but Anchises always praised us for being the two fastest runners. Then he would send us to run down to the harbor and back again, as punishment or praise, I could not tell.

On the sparring field, Hector often found me. The other boys more or less fought amongst themselves, still not quite comfortable at training alongside girls. Especially the flame-haired boy — who I discovered was named Paris and who was sullen about everyone and everything — avoided fighting with my Amazon companions. But Hector never feared us, even when I managed to best him a few times and land him solidly upon his backside in the practice sands. He always laughed and wiped himself off, then rose again for another bout. I found I could not hold a grudge against him, even when fate found me on the ground with his winning blade held up to my throat. Anchises praised us both in equal measure, and I felt my abilities growing in stride with the prince's.

Hippolyta excelled too, and I felt closer to her again than I had in those last few months at home before leaving for Ilium. We spent the days together, surrounded by our friends, throwing our bodies into the peaceful exertion of exhaustion, then spent our nights huddled up in the common room, singing with the other girls over dinner and wine. After some time, a few of the boys, Hector, of course, and some of his brothers, began to join us in our evening carouse — always carefully shooed out by the grandmotherly servants assigned to our barracks before the nights got too friendly.

It was a peaceful time, though we were learning the arts of war.

One day, Anchises was called to King Priam for counsel, and our training was canceled. A few of us girls escaped the city and followed a trail west down to the banks of the little river that drew a line south from the bay and through the various pastures encircling Ilium. Lyta had chosen to stay behind, though I trusted her enough at this point to have overcome my fear of her randomly courting some idiotic prince and falling pregnant by him, so I nodded to her and left with the others. Hector and Aeneas decided to join us, though poor, pale Aeneas seemed to come along only because of his cousin's insistence.

The sun glared down at us like always, but when we reached the little river, we found its waters just cool enough to be refreshing. Aeneas was the first to dive in, probably to soothe his red, burning skin. The girls laughed as he came up, sputtering at how cold the water was! We all dunked either our whole selves or just our toes to make him feel silly. Truly, the water wasn't as cold as all that.

Hector pulled me aside while the others splashed and played with each other. He had a serious look on his plain face, and the water weighed down his dark curls to hang over his furrowed brow. I flicked water at him and laughed when he flinched with surprise. We sat beside each other a little way down the river from the Aeneas and the girls in the shade of an olive tree that also served to mask us a little from sight.

"What is it?" I asked. Hector knew me to be blunt and never bemoaned it in the past.

He looked down at his feet, bare since he had left his sandals further down the river. "My father told me something, Pen." He looked very grave and not at all like the carefree youth he often played to me and Lyta. Though he was serious, I felt a little stir of joy to hear him use my sister's pet name for me.

"Hector, whatever it is, you just have to tell me. Is King Priam going to send us back home? We haven't finished training here yet. Does he want us all gone?"

"He wants me to marry." Hector cut through my questions like a bronze blade through a shield of cheese.

"What?"

Hector squirmed beside me. "My father wants me to get married. He says it's my duty as his son and heir. I—I didn't know what to tell him. Of course, I knew he would make me someday, but I never thought . . ." His words drifted off, and he gazed up at me with all the fear of disappointing his father that I often felt about myself and Otrera.

"Oh, Hector," I said, reaching out to grab his hand.

In a moment, he leaned forwards, and I found his lips pressing against mine in an unwanted kiss. I reared back and pushed myself up to the trunk of the olive tree.

"What are you doing?" I sputtered. I was not often lost for words, but here was quite the moment.

Hector's face turned bright red. "I thought—that is," he sputtered, losing all hope at civilized language. "I thought you wanted me to...."

My eyes widened. "Well, no...."

"Oh, gods!" Poor Hector buried his head in his hands. "I'm sorry! It's just—you're a girl and a princess, and the other boys said we should, well, you know, unite, so to speak, and

I feel so close to you, and...."

I didn't know who I felt more mortified for, myself or my bright red companion. "None of that matters now, does it," I said, cutting him off from saying anything else foolish. "Do you...do you love me?" I asked, almost afraid to know his answer.

My question didn't make him any less bashful, but at least it caused his brain to revive itself. He pursed his lips and pondered the idea for a while. By that very fact, I thought I knew his answer, but I kept my silence.

"I—" he began, "I don't know exactly. You're my friend, my best friend, and we like all the same things and do all the same things together, and you're a girl, and I'm a boy...does that make us in love?"

I shook my head, trying to look as worldly and knowledgeable as someone with no knowledge whatsoever on the subject at hand. "Hector, none of that means you love me. It doesn't even mean you should love me. Anyway, I think love is something you're sure about. Maybe we just have a friendly kind of love between us, the way good comrades have." I held back my tongue from mentioning that I had no interest in loving anyone, at least not physically, and not the way he meant.

Hector seemed to consider my words deeply. When he was done, he looked a little relieved. "Well, in that case, I'm a bit glad, if I'm being honest. I mean, of course, I like you—you're closer to me than my heart—but I hadn't really decided that I loved you, I suppose." He smiled, some of his regular color returning. "I feel awfully foolish now, Pen. Please forget all that. And don't tell your sister; she'll mock me mercilessly."

I laughed, sure that he was right about Lyta's reaction. "Of course. But Hector, what is this about Priam wanting you to wed? He didn't mean to me, right?"

Hector shook his head, sending water flying from his curls. "No, that was part of it. He wants me to marry some girl I've never met before. He said her name is Andromache or something. But I don't want to marry her! And not just because I thought maybe you and I should wed. I just don't know that I'm ready for it. All of Ilium seems to want me crowned heir apparent. I just want to be me."

I bit my lip. What was there for me to say? What words of mine could salve the heartache of my poor friend? Perhaps Otrera or Hippolyta, in their charismatic ways, might know what to do, but I could offer no such consolation. I simply sat with Hector on the banks of the little river, trying to forget he was bound to be king of the huge city behind us and I was bound to be queen of warriors.

Chapter 11 - πόλεμος

THE WAR

The tent of Achilles arched behind the smaller tents and structures of his Myrmidon soldiers. The Myrmidons stood apart from the other Argives, more disciplined than the wilder men carousing through the camp. I wondered again at how these apparent bumblers could have brought Ilium to its knees for so long. Ilium, the greatest city in the world. Ilium, the home of heroes.

But, of course, the Argives had their own men they called heroes, and here was one of them now.

I spat in the sand. Achilles was no hero. He was a man — no, he was less than a man, more animal, more beast than a human creature. He was lawless, godless, and worthless. My mind spun with unsworn obscenities.

But no, I was here to follow Priam. And so I forced down all my thoughts of revenge and murder and turned back to my chosen task. The king of Ilium crept like a sneak thief past the Myrmidon tents, staying as far out of the light of the men's bonfires and torches as possible, becoming nothing more than a slinking beggar. I wrapped the darkened cloak tighter around me, transforming myself into a shadowy wraith at the heels of the king. Apparently, supplicants were a usual sight at the tent of Achilles, and the Myrmidons barely spared us a glance as we approached.

Just to the right of the entrance to Achilles' tent lay the unholy reminder of Priam's woe: the body of Hector.

Naked but for blood and sand and the passing blade of grass, Hector sprawled before the tent. Here was no corpse prepared by priests to face the gods. Here no robe or winding sheet wrapped the body. Here no oils had been pressed into the once-supple skin. Priam's son was twisted, discarded like an old cloak, dropped to the floor and forgotten. His hair was matted, and abrasions on his face and body were black and horrible. At the corpse's heels, two slices had been made, and a line of rope fed through them so that Achilles might drag his fallen foe through further indignity.

Priam saw his son and blanched. He nearly collapsed at Hector's side, and I still thought he might fall there to die himself at the side of his son. The king breathed deeply, and he stared hard at Hector. Where was the Hector who'd impressed me all those years ago with his bright, shining honor and his loyal friendship? Where was the Hector who had shown me and Lyta respect, even though we were women? Where was the Hector who I had known? Where was Priam's son? Surely, he could not have been brought down so easily. Surely, the warrior I'd befriended would never die at the hands of some contemptible Argive. Surely, my friend could not be this small, mortal corpse slumped on enemy sands. Surely, Hector still lived. Surely, surely.

I, who had seen corpses before — I, who had won battles before and strewn numerous bodies upon the battlefield — I could not stand to look at the corpse of Hector. My whole body trembled as if I saw my own corpse there. No—as if I saw Hippolyta's. The open face of Hector with its half-gaping mouth full of flies became my beautiful Lyta, the twisted shoulders those of my sister now instead of Hector. My body trembled, and I staggered into a pit of shadow to the other side of the entrance. I sucked in breath after breath but could not get enough. My head buzzed, and my vision blurred. Why could I not breathe? Poor Hector, oh, poor Hippolyta—gods, poor Priam!

How the King of Ilium managed to stay afoot, I could not say, but when I looked up, I saw a man approach him from Achilles' tent. I hesitated, not sure how much involvement to have in this bizarre situation. Priam, speaking to the man, threw back his shoulders and gestured to his cart of ransom. The man appeared momentarily shocked before he recovered himself and waved Priam onwards.

Priam was through the draped entrance to the tent before I could step in. I cursed and swept around to the side of the tent. Here I was, dithering in the shadows while the King of Ilium, the most important leader in this war, was off to meet his greatest enemy! I slipped around the outside of the tent until I was deep in the shadows, hidden from even the sharpest of Myrmidon's eyes. Then I knelt and slid my dagger out to cut a small slit in the thick canvas sailcloth of the tent wall.

Achilles, a hulking figure, backlit by a small hearth.

Priam, hands spread as if to plead.

The greatest men of this war, meeting at last.

I pressed my eye up to the slit I'd made and sucked in a breath.

This was the closest I had been to the monster Achilles.

I stared as King Priam knelt before him, royal raiments pushed into the sandy ground of Achilles' tent. Achilles loomed over him like a hulking creature ready to pounce. The hero of the Argives was tall, taller than I had imagined, even taller than me or Hector, who had been tall in life. Unlike the lithe Hector, the body of Achilles was thick and bulky with muscle. As he pivoted and stepped back from Priam, more of the monster's face became visible, and the light of the hearth and the torches near the entryway burnished his golden hair, almost red and firelike itself. His face was creased with lines from stress, not age. His eyes were shadowed under strong brows. His cheek, naked as a woman's—not bearded like many of his counterparts. His lips twisted downwards wryly. Wearing only a short chiton, it was clear he went unarmored and unarmed.

So this was Achilles.

I pictured myself slitting his throat. His blood ran in torrents over my hands.

The hero of the Argives, the killer of Hector, sank onto a stool and closed his eyes.

Priam pressed his hands into the sand. His cheeks shone wet with tears. He stared at Achilles, then lowered his head to the ground as well. Groveling. Begging. A king begging before a beast.

Achilles did not raise his eyes to look at the king of Ilium.

For several moments, nothing moved in the tent besides the flickering flames, and I feared even my breathing might be too loud for this silent, morose encounter. But then Achilles sighed, a sound so loud I thought perhaps he had been holding his breath too.

"Speak, king," intoned Achilles. He sounded weary. Probably tired from his warring and murdering. Monster. I seethed against the bonds of my own making—how dishonorable would it be to sneak into the enemy camp and assassinate even the least honorable fighters in the Argive army? I could not break the hide-bound ways of warfare, no matter how much I wanted to. Achilles would die on the battlefield or not by my hand.

The King of Ilium dug his fingers into the sand. "This earth was mine," he began, his voice coming out in hesitant spurts. "This was my land, my kingdom, my legacy. Now all I have is the great walled city of Ilium." His small body shook with sobs.

Achilles stared at him. "Ilium is not so small a prize, king."

Priam continued as though he hadn't heard Achilles' retort. "I am king of many, but to fewer now since the Argives arrived at my shores. And I was father to many—but to fewer sons now than—" he choked on sobs.

"Fewer than before?" Achilles supplied. "Yes, and there were more Argives too. You see their tombs along the shoreline." I seethed at the bitter note in his voice. He turned his face from Priam, and the hint of firelight painted a yellow glow along his jawline. He frowned. "We've all been here too long," he said, almost to no one.

But Priam lifted his hands from the sands then and straightened his back as well as he could. "I've lost many sons before this day, son of Peleus," he said to Achilles, "but you have killed the greatest of them. You have...you have slain my beloved Hector." He stared at Achilles until the younger Argive was forced to turn back and lock eyes with him.

"Aye, and who killed Patroclus?" The air was still. Achilles hissed the name again, this time saying, "My Patroclus."

"I don't deny that Hector killed Patroclus," said Priam, his voice now stone. "But this is war! Patroclus wore your armor. Bore your weapons! He was no milkmaid in a field, fallen on by sneaking warriors. He stood against the greatest son of Ilium. He wanted to fight!" Priam's voice may have calmed, but new tears fell fresh from his eyes. "And you got him back—we allowed you that honor. You've been able to mourn him as is your right."

"I've been mourning all my life, old man."

Achilles's words struck me like a physical blow. They were words I might have said, words I had certainly thought many times, especially since the tragedy of Hippolyta. Especially since I learned the true secrets of living as a warrior. You could spend every day mourning your losses if you let yourself. How odd to find someone like Achilles, someone for whom hate burned like the torch of Prometheus in my breast, putting my own thoughts into words.

"Think of—" stammered Priam. "Think of your own father. Think of his love for you. Think of his desire for you to return from this siege. Great Peleus still has a hope that you will return to him. Great Peleus might yet see his son again. But here I am, father to no one, father to a corpse. And even that corpse is refused me! All I want is to mourn him in the proper ways. To lay him to rest." His crinkled old face looked thin as paper in the firelight, his body narrow enough to crush with one hand and little effort. He was a dead man, still walking and talking and breathing, but nearer to death than the shades in Hades.

Achilles looked at his hands. He'd placed them, palms down, on his knees. From my distance, his hands appeared to tremble, though it could have been the trick of the light.

"Mourning him will not bring him back. Trust me." He glanced over to a pile of armor. The armor of Patroclus, I guessed, from how reverently it had been cleaned and arranged.

"No, I know that," choked out Priam, "but just give me the chance." He bent forwards again. "I have brought ransom, the riches of my city, all for you if you let me leave here with my son's body." He gestured a gnarled hand at his cart.

I didn't like the look in Achilles' eyes, but I also found his face, his whole person, entirely impossible to read. What did he think within that handsome, vile face of his? Did he feel as we humans did? Did he understand any of the grief old Priam had shared with him? From what I had heard of the warrior, I did not imagine him capable. From what I had witnessed atop the walls of Ilium, I knew him only to be cruel. But here he sat, without armor or walls of his own, hands trembling before the grief of Priam.

The enemies stared hard at each other for some time. My impatience shook me, and I nearly rose and made to enter the tent when Achilles himself stood. "Alkimos!" he cried. One of the pair of men from before barged in, bowing before his friend and master. "Untie the body of Hector and bring it here. Bring water and oils." My muscles tensed, but I remained frozen at my vantage point. Priam gazed at Achilles, trying to parse his thoughts, but couldn't.

"Do you mean to give him to me?" The old king's voice was so small he could barely be heard over the guttering of the flames as Alkimos left the tent.

Before Achilles replied, in strode a servant girl whose bearing belied a higher birth. "Briseis, you will help me clean the body and prepare it as is right," he commanded.

"As we did for Patroclus, my lord." She bowed.

Alkimos returned then, the body of Hector carried between him and another, larger man. They set him down in the center of the chamber. Priam rose slightly and staggered over to his son's body. In the firelight, Hector seemed almost alive, like his chest rose and fell with breath, and his eyes might just flicker open to stare around himself. A deep, low moan came from Priam's throat and from his very soul indeed as he knelt by Hector. Since the slaying, he had not been so close to his son. Tears crinkled my own eyes as I saw the old man reach out a tentative hand to clasp that of his son. He held the dirty, pale fingers in his hand until Achilles approached and, with shocking tenderness, placed his strong hands on the king's shoulders.

"Come, old father," he said, "sit back and let us clean him as befits the prince of Ilium." Priam went and curled beside the hearth like a twice-beaten dog.

Breathlessly, I watched as Achilles and Briseis carefully cleansed the body. The serving girl brought in pails of water, which they gently poured over the corpse, once and twice over. Clean rags wiped away the dirt and blood, and other detritus left there from Achilles' rides across the battlefield. The girl ran her fingers through Hector's hair, combing out any dirt from there as well. Then Achilles knelt beside her to hand her a jar of pungent oils, which she massaged into the graying flesh. Wherever rot or injury had raised an imperfection, Achilles himself bound a strip of white cloth over the region, whispering a prayer into each wrap. When their work was done, Achilles took from his own stock a cloak of the deepest indigo, which the two bundled around the body. Then Achilles knelt before the covered face of Hector.

"Forgive me, Patroclus," he said, his voice so low I was shocked to have heard it. Then he kissed Hector's forehead and turned to Priam. "It is done," he said. "You may take him from here, unmolested by the Argives."

"You have done me the greatest honor," replied Priam, trying to stand. But his body quaked beneath him, and he tumbled back onto the ground.

Achilles rushed to the king's side and half-lifted him into his arms. "You are tired, old man." He stared hard at the king, but with his back mostly to me, I could make out no expression on his face—not that I could have understood it were he facing me. This man was an enigma, to be sure. "Let yourself rest here for a time and leave just before the sun rises."

I feared treachery, but Priam simply nodded. "Place me beside my son," he said. Achilles nodded and settled the king next to the body of Hector. Priam reached out a bony hand and wrapped it tightly around his son's forearm. "Now I can rest," he said, before laying down his head and falling almost instantly asleep.

Briseis busied herself with making ready for the night while Achilles crouched by the old king for a time.

Finally, I moved back from the slit in the tent I'd made and sat myself upon the ground. Out of the light of the tent, the rest of the Argive camp had turned dark and languid, asleep even as Priam was. I felt restive. How could sleep take hold of so many so fast? My mind and body raced, and I found myself pacing in the small space between the Myrmidon tents. I supposed that Achilles and his servant and the rest of his men would sleep too. I alone would lie awake, puzzling together the strange things I had just witnessed. The version of Achilles I had seen within this tent did not mesh with my vision from the walls of Troy. Could it be that there were two Achilles, just as there were two Penthesileas — one who slaughtered a leopard to save her sister and one who wept over the leopard's death each night afterwards?

A noise from one of the tents snapped my attention back up. A man emerged from the shadows behind Achilles' tent, his torso bare and hands empty but for a small torch in his right hand. He stared at me without moving for a time.

"Who are you?" asked Achilles, son of Peleus, slayer of Hector.

Chapter 12 - ἔρως

LOVE

Training at Ilium became a dream from which I never wished to wake. The camaraderie between my Amazons and me, my growing friendship with Hector, and even earning the respect and praise of curmudgeonly Anchises—all these lifted my spirits higher than ever before. Of course, I missed Otrera and life on our island. But I had never known my heart to be as full as it was in Ilium.

Occasionally Priam would descend from his garish palace to the practice fields to cheer on his many sons, always favoring Hector. I thrilled to see my friend praised so, for he truly was the best of the royal sons, better at all aspects of fighting but also magnanimous in his wins. Even his brothers, who found themselves losing to him time and time again, could never hold grudges, for he cheered for them until his voice grew hoarse whenever he watched them spar, and he was always willing to help clean and polish armor with his brothers and half-brothers. He had even been known to drive a chariot for his youngest siblings, though we all knew that in a real fight, he would be the spear-caster. The respect and deference shown Hector seemed to cascade onto us Amazons, and most of the sons of Priam treated us with dignity and honor.

Most of the sons of Priam.

One of Hector's younger brothers, the one called Paris, still regarded us as interlopers and afforded us the barest scraps of courtesy necessitated by our station. Anchises appeared to notice and, many months into our sojourn in Ilium, forced the contention into one of his practice sessions.

Anchises assigned two warlords for our games the next day — his own son, Aeneas, and Paris. The warlords were allowed to divide the rest of the group into their two sides and strategize together for the upcoming mock battle. Aeneas had chosen all the Amazons, as well as Hector and a good deal of the palace boys, while Paris came away with the rest. Of course, both sides had argued over who would get Hector, but Paris seemed pleased to let Aeneas handle the girls. And so Hector, Aeneas, Hippolyta, and I were tucked around the hearth fire in the Amazon's common room long after the sun had set, discussing strategies and chariot pairings.

Aeneas had grown up in just the matter of months I'd known, cleared his throat and sipped at his watery wine. His skin had finally accepted the sunlight and started to tan rather than burn. He was handsome now, I supposed, and more than a few of the girls in my care liked to grin and primp at him to throw him off-balance. Still shy, it often worked in a sparring match to the girls' advantage.

Hector marked out simple battle lines on a piece of slate in his lap. "We can fortify this hummock here," he was saying, "and send our chariots out with the river to our left. That way, we only have one line of attack to worry about." Our wargames were set to take place in a fallow field outside the city.

Hippolyta shook her head. "And if they attack so hard they push us into the river?" She wiped away a bit of Hector's slate markings. "Then the horses and chariots will be bogged down in muddy waters."

"I suppose you're right," conceded Hector. "What about—" He was cut off by a banging at the entrance.

In strode Paris, his eyes a little red from drinking. He had grown up like Aeneas, but he still had the flame-red hair and sullen face I remembered from our first meeting.

"So this is how Hector and Aeneas spend their time with women, eh?" he crowed and staggered his way deeper into our chamber. "Curled up before a fire reciting tactics? Did you even know what else you can do with a warm, little woman in the dark of night?"

Hector and Aeneas both rose, anger smudging their faces.

"Those words are not appropriate for our company, Paris," said Hector. His voice was clear and demanding.

Paris simply laughed. "That's what girls are for, brother! Perhaps dumb Aeneas here should spend more time with someone who actually knows how to take pleasure with a woman!"

Aeneas turned pink up to his ears.

Hippolyta and I rose behind our two friends.

"You wouldn't know pleasure if it reached up and bit your dick," spat Hippolyta.

The drunken stupor slid from Paris' face, and he glared at my sister like his very eyes might strike her down. "I don't need to be insulted by some whore girl whose mother was in love with my father!" Spit flew from his mouth as he spoke.

"I don't need to listen to some dickless nobody! You'll never have the respect of any man, not one that doesn't want to fuck you!"

I was flying at Paris before he was even done speaking. His insults were too much to bear, too great a weight to be asked to ignore any longer. I reached him and closed my hands around his scrawny neck. His fists flew against my torso, and I grunted with pain. Lyta appeared at my side, her arms wrapping around me and trying to pull me off him. Hector and Aeneas flew to Paris and did the same with him. Soon we were pulled apart, though neither of us stopped trying to escape their grasps and mesh together with punches and kicks.

"All you whores are the same!" shouted Paris. "You're all just lonely, man-crazed witches who can't get a real man to bed you."

Hector let go of Paris and struck him across the face. At that, the younger boy staggered back and quieted. Outside the practice fields, the brothers were not allowed to strike one another, a rule of Priam's that was constantly obeyed. Hector stood over his brother, his hands curling into fists and uncurling over and over.

"Speak ill of our guests once more, Paris," said Hector, "and I won't stop them from tearing your dick off and feeding it to the pigs."

Paris stared up at his brother. Blood dribbled from his nose and onto his full lips. He looked like he might speak, might howl his outrage at Hector, might once again insult the honor of Hippolyta and myself. But he didn't. He wiped away the blood and rose and stumped from the common room.

Aeneas and Hippolyta fussed over me to make sure I

wasn't injured, but Hector and I locked eyes without speaking. Paris was a problem, for me, for Hector, and possibly for all of Ilium.

The battle Anchises had set for us went as well as could be expected. Early that morning, Paris claimed ill health and ceded his position to his brother Deiphobus. Under the bright morning sun, Deiphobus and Hector deployed their chariots like expert generals, each leading their own charge. Hector held us Amazons back at first to release us a surprise when the enemy closed in, thinking they had won. This wave of our attack had been discussed only between Hector and myself and me and my women. So much of the strategy depended on surprising our attackers.

Deiphobus led an admirable charge, his brothers and cousins fighting better than they would have under the direction of Paris. His chariots rumbled against ours, and the boys cast blunted spears at our drivers and casters. The two sides seemed almost equal in skill and maneuverability.

Then Hector sounded his horn, our secret signal. My Amazons and I burst from our hiding spot in a nearby vineyard and thundered against the open rear flank of Deiphobus' force. The chariot riders tried to turn, but they were too cumbersome and slow.

We, on the other hand, could fly in and strike, swooping in like hawks on a field of mice. We rode no chariots pulled by a team of horses. We sat astride the horses themselves, squeezing our knees about their girths so we wouldn't fall, and cast our spears from horseback. We decimated the retreating charioteers, and the battle ended when I struck Deiphobus on the helmet with a soft-tipped javelin.

Anchises, striding down from his viewpoint on a nearby rise, applauded Hector's work as a general.

"And you, girls—no, Amazon warriors," he said, facing me and Hippolyta and the other sweat-stained and battle-worn women, "I've never seen a charge quite like that. Ilium is lucky to count you among its allies."

After that, our status was greatly improved. Though no one had outwardly insulted us before—except Paris—the feeling of most military men was that women did not belong on a battlefield unless she was a healer and the fighting was already over. Now, however, we filled out a new category amongst the populace of Ilium, a new position for women which had never existed before. The allowances given us Amazon women only stood for us, though, not the women of Ilium. It was almost like we were no longer women, but some mysterious other that had been accepted by Priam, and the people accepted but not understood.

Paris recovered from his bout of ill health but refused to rejoin the training with Anchises. He alone among all the people of Ilium bore for us a seething hatred. But, as he grew more foppish in his palace, his spite became easier to ignore.

All too soon, our training was over. The days had raced by, but Lyta reminded me that we had been gone from Otrera's island for over a year. I considered my muscles, the knowledge of warfare and tactics I'd developed, and my deep friendship with Hector—and it could have been a year or a lifetime we'd been at Ilium. I realized that I did not want to leave. It would be like leaving Otrera's island all over again, for this had become another home to me. I knew the other girls felt the same. Some of them, despite my best efforts, had fallen in love with a few of Priam's sons or cousins. This would be their first taste of heartbreak.

Hector met us at the entrance to our barracks the morning we were set to leave. Saying goodbye to him would be my first taste of heartbreak, too, though not in quite the same way as the other girls. We stood eye to eye, for we were both exceedingly tall, and I could see the start of tears in his dark eyes.

We hugged, not as lovers but as dear, dear friends.

"How do I know if I'll ever see you again, Pen?" he asked, not bothering to cover the hitch in his voice. Hector was so sensitive for a warrior, brave as well as caring, a quality I thought would serve him well whenever Priam died and he became King of Ilium.

"I'm sure I'll come back here again," I said. I wasn't sure of any such thing. But I did feel strongly that I had not seen my last glimpse of Priam's great city yet.

Hector took my calloused hands in his and squeezed them as if he never wanted to let go. "I will miss you. You are the best friend I've known." He smiled, a little slyly. "I love you better than all my brothers, you know."

I laughed at him. "Your brothers are all so bothersome — that's not saying much." But I squeezed his hands back. "But there are so many of them, so I know you compliment me. I love you just as much as I love Lyta."

Then he laughed at me. "I should have known I could never compete with your darling sister!" He released me and waved me across the small yard before our barracks. "Come, I have a gift for you."

My eyes narrowed. "What sort of gift?" But I was already following him out into the yard.

Hector marched up to a horse with the most beautiful golden coat and warm, auburn eyes. "He's yours," he said, patting the horse's gleaming neck.

I could barely breathe. The horse was like a statue burnished in gold, so elegant and strong, with long legs and stout muscles. He tossed his yellow mane as I ran my fingers along his coat, feeling his heat and power.

"Hector," I gasped. "He's — "

My friend smiled at me. "He is yours. You must think of me every time you ride him and know that I am thinking about you and remembering all the time we spent together." His eyes crinkled, and tears finally did slide down his tanned cheeks.

We embraced again and discussed the horse, and embraced and laughed, and trotted the palomino about the yard. "I shall call him Zephyr after the winds that will carry our greetings to each other, even when we are separated." I cried a little, too, though not as much as Hector, and we both had to clean our faces to make ourselves presentable for the march down to the shore and the ships that would take us home again.

In a direct reversal of our first appearance at Ilium, Priam led a massive entourage back down to the bay. Instead of splitting into separate groups, however, the sons of Priam and the Amazons walked intermixed as friends and comrades now rather than strangers. I led Zephyr at the front of the group of youths, and Hector walked on the horse's other side. Lyta strode beside Anchises, who seemed more than a little sad to see us leaving his care.

At the shore, Hector embraced me again, which was sure to stir up rumors again of a love between us. We barely cared. He said goodbye to Lyta and each of the other Amazons. Priam let us go with only a short lecture on being allies and bade us to greet Otrera with his words of love and friendship.

The ships pulled away from the little harbor. I watched Hector stand with his feet in the water, cerulean waves lapping around his ankles, waving to us until he became nothing more than a dot on the shoreline. I waved back at him and knew I would never again have so great friend. Lyta, at my side as always, waved right along with me, but her dreamy eyes were already moving on somewhere else.

Themyscira, as Priam had named it, was a world in chaos when we returned. The little village I remembered had grown and been fortified since we had left — and it had been over a year now, almost a year and a half, by the gods — and I barely recognized the place. There was a real port now, with wooden docks and low buildings straddling the beach, an actual road that led through the trees into the village proper — it was as if we had landed on a different island.

But the women we met there welcomed us as if we'd been gone only an afternoon. It was a warm homecoming, to say the least.

And yet there was trouble because Otrera was not at the dock to greet us. Apparently, she had hurt her leg so badly that she could no longer put any weight on it. Hippolyta and I rushed back to our home to see her.

I'd never seen Mother look so fragile, laying on a couch like an invalid. But her face was bright and brightened further upon seeing us.

"My beautiful queens!" she exclaimed as we fell into

her open arms. "How much you have grown." She held us close to her for a moment, savoring the touch and feel of us, daughters whom she had not seen but sorely missed. We did the same with her, though gently, so as not to hurt her. "There are so many questions I have for you both," she said, "and so much I want to hear about. But first, there is someone I want you to meet."

She gestured at the open doorway, and a man came striding in. The man had chestnut brown hair and was somewhere between the ages of my mother and me, closer, I thought to Otrera's years. He bowed to us all with equal deference. Lyta and I straightened, and something in my heart lurched to see a man on our island where none had been allowed for so long.

"This is an emissary from another kingdom," said Otrera. "He is a friend. His name is Theseus, King of Athens."

Chapter 13 - πόλεμος

THE WAR

I tossed the cloak back, revealing my leopard skin. "I am Penthesilea," I answered. "Queen of the Amazons." My dagger leapt into my hand. Achilles brandished his torch like the strongest bronze sword, and we clashed together behind the tents.

My blood ran hotter through my veins than I could remember, and at last, I felt like the daughter of a god. My enemy's golden body writhed just out of reach of my blade as I myself side-stepped his every thrust with the torch. A small cloud of sand kicked up around our feet. Achilles sucked in a deep breath and kicked one bare foot against my cuirass, striking the heavy metal. Though unwounded, the blow jarred me, and I teetered backwards. He tried to press his advantage, but though I could barely breathe, I flashed my dagger from left to right and sliced his torch in half. The fiery end tumbled to the ground and petered out to nothing more than an ember.

Our tight field of battle turned dark, and we both flew back to gather our wits and senses. From the darkness, a low chuckle emerged. Color rose in my cheeks.

"Why do you laugh at me, Argive?" I spat.

"You have chosen quite the metaphor to emasculate me, warrior woman." I could just see him gesture with the leftover torch. "Not quite how I like my women."

"I'm not another Helen nor some whore to play with in the night. I'll kill you like you killed Hector." I could barely see him but sensed that he grew still.

"So again, we come to the prince of Ilium," he intoned. "I see. I shall pay the price for that for the rest of my days."

"Maybe you won't have long to worry about that."

To my surprise, Achilles dropped the rest of his makeshift weapon and sat upon the ground. "Have you heard my sad prophecy as well, then?" An errant cloud undraped itself from before the moon just then and bathed us both in clear, sacred light. I stared down at Achilles, my great enemy. He sat cross-legged like a child before me with his face upturned towards mine. I clenched my teeth so hard I could have ripped a man's arm off had it been between my jaws. Achilles stared up at me like a child — or like a supplicant, like Priam had to him only hours ago.

"What prophecy?" I asked, never loosening my grip on my dagger.

"My mother is a goddess, you know," he said, flatly. "She tells me I can either live a long life without prestige or die young with the fame of a god." He closed his eyes, and weariness settled on his moonlit features. "Can you guess which I chose?"

I stared at him. How he held his neck, it would be so easy to slit just then, to revenge myself on the slayer of Hector. I could tear through his jugular and let him bleed out on the sands that rightfully belonged to Ilium. But if old Priam had not taken that chance himself, had ostensibly forgiven this beast or made peace, at least, by what greater right could I claim his life? But all deaths must be avenged! My mind argued. It cried and rocked and screamed against me as I sank to the sand and sheathed my blade. Still, I stared at Achilles as if daring him to make a wrong move or word. I could still kill him. And he could kill me. We both knew it.

But this was not the battlefield between Ilium and the Argives. This was merely a back-alley scuffle. Neither of us would die here. We both knew that too.

"So," I said. There was an edge to my voice that I had no wish to soothe. "You chose fame and glory over a long life. And all those you have slain are left with neither."

He did not shake his head, but the lines on his face deepened at my words. "I don't argue your point, Queen of Women. But we are both warriors. You know how it is to fight and slay your enemies. It is always a choice of your own death over theirs. And I do not yet choose to die."

Yet. The word hung between us like a pall, closing in from all sides.

"How do you think you will die?" I asked, my voice grown quiet at last.

"I know I will die on the field of battle," he replied. He traced some symbols, barely visible in the sands between us. "I had hoped it would be at the hands of Hector."

I scoffed. "Sure. And that is why you sank your blade into his belly and let him die while his own father and mother watched from the walls." I was appalled. His charade of regret should not have won me over so easily. I started to rise.

"When he killed Patroclus, he took from me my heart." Achilles' voice stopped me from standing, though he was quiet as a fieldmouse. "When they brought me back Patroclus' body, oh, how I wept. He was—no, is, is is is, and always—my dearest love. I wanted to die then." He stopped his sand-scrawling, lost in the memories of his dead friend. "I have wished death upon myself for each and every day since then. I wished for it when I woke that morning. I wished it when I stood before Hector with our blades crossing. I wished it when he stared out at me from beneath his helmet and died at my feet."

This was something I had not expected—a penitent monster. "Then why did you kill him?" I asked at last. "Why not let him win? There would be no shame in losing to great Hector." I considered my words carefully before I added, "I trained with him when we were young. He was a great warrior even then."

He smiled and snorted ruefully. "When you live your life as a warrior, when all your life people tell you how to fight and how to kill, it is not an easy thing to let yourself be killed, even by a hero like Hector."

"Do not mock him with the word 'hero' when you have treated him so poorly," I hissed.

He brushed away the mystery symbols in the sand with a violent gesture. "I should not have done that," he admitted.

"Well?" I flicked sand into his lap, and he jerked back a little, startled. "Why did you? Do you not have common sense in the half-godly head of yours? Have none of you Argives ever learned decency? Does self-control get taught to your heroes?"

"I am not a hero, Penthesilea. I am a man."

"You just said you were birthed to a goddess. Does that not make you more than a man?" I argued.

"Perhaps it makes me less of one."

Somewhere in the camp, a dog barked. Another one yipped into the night in response, and soon the whole camp was flooded with the noisy rumblings of canines.

"I killed my sister." The words came out before I knew it, before I understood I was speaking. Achilles stared into my eyes, and I felt strangely unburdened by my omission, even though I hated him so, so much. He did not take my hands or try to hold me as another man might, as I had seen men comfort women in the past. Always physical, always dominating them in some way. But Achilles simply nodded and waited for me to continue.

The words, the whole story, pressed at my throat like a roaring river. I sat with my mouth clamped as long as I could before the tale unwound itself from the shoals of my mind. "My sister, Hippolyta. She was a fighter like me, but she became someone's wife. I wanted her to be happy, but he betrayed her. And so I led my warriors to attack him in his citadel. I was one blow away from killing him—I had brought him to his knees." I paused, revisiting the scene in my mind for the hundredth, no the thousandth time. "Poor Lyta. Even in her cuckolding, she could not watch me kill her husband. And so she stepped in front of my blade and took the thrust that was meant for him." I closed my eyes, seeing her blood jetting against my hand and staining my wrist, a red ocean— endless, endless. "I meant to avenge her. I meant to punish him for hurting her." I opened my eyes and looked down at my own empty hands. "But I failed. And I have dishonored myself more than anyone else ever could."

Achilles stared at me, his face lacking the judgment I saw even in the eyes of my woman companions.

"I see Lyta in the face of every man I kill here. I keep thinking that...that if I fight for Ilium, if I kill the right enemies, maybe the gods will forgive me. But I can never...." I choked on the words, ones thought but had never spoken before aloud. "But I can never forgive myself." I bowed my head. All the longing and regret, and grief swirled within my head in a potent melange.

"As I cannot forgive myself," added Achilles after many breaths of silence. "I see Patroclus around every corner, in every stranger's face. I saw him in Hector, even as I dishonored his body." He, too, drew quiet. "Perhaps we are not meant to forgive ourselves. Perhaps we will never earn forgiveness, not even from the gods, but maybe it wasn't supposed to come to us like that. We are warriors, Penthesilea."

I waved my hand to encompass all the men of the Argive camp and the city of Ilium as well. "They are all warriors! Should none of us earn forgiveness for any of it?"

Achilles shrugged. "Maybe not. Maybe none of this is what the gods want of us." He drew a circle between us in the sand. "But, Penthesilea, do not make the mistake of thinking you are equal to these common soldiers, either here or in Ilium."

"Why?" I bridled. "Because I am a woman? Because I am lesser than even the drunkest, most loutish of men?"

Laughing, truly laughing, Achilles threw back his head. "Lesser? Gods, Penthesilea, but you are mightier than all us men put together!" His smile glowed in the moonlight, brighter and more cheerful than I had expected. "Men follow orders—orders from commanders, from kings, from gods. We follow our proscribed paths through age and old age and death. Even I obey the prophecy of my birth. But you, what

fate do you follow? Whose orders do you obey?" He looked
at me and stared deep into my eyes.

For a moment, I stared back at him. His eyes were
blue, almost silver in the light of the moon, the symbol of my
goddess. I considered his words. Did all men merely follow
the strands of fate until they fell victim to their ultimate
mortality? I certainly had not felt that way. I simply did as
I wished or as I felt was right, whatever the outcome might
be. Was Achilles right about me, then? Did I somehow reach
above the lives of men and choose my own path? But then
why did I feel so confused, so flustered, so lacking in purpose
now? Ever since Lyta's death, I had no direction, no aim, no
goal. Then Priam summoned me to Ilium, and I had centered
all my hopes around the singular purpose of rescuing the
city. But perhaps this was just another stone in the path I had
before me, the path of my life.

Could I cut the string of fate that I'd refused to follow
and untether myself completely from these worldly woes?

Would that mean my death? Was death something I
could accept?

My breath hitched. If it meant being reunited with
Hippolyta, with Hector, with all those dead and gone before
me—maybe.

But, then again, I'd never been one to obey the gods.
Maybe I would never reunite with my fallen family. Maybe
I would live—continue to live—and find a new purpose for
myself.

Achilles began to tell me then about Patroclus. About
the gleam of sunlight in his hair and his brash behavior. Then he
told me of his own life. About his childhood on Mount Pelion
and later Phthia. He sounded so like me talking endlessly

of my own adventures with Hippolyta that I laughed and wept at the same time. I told him of our adventure with the leopard and our youths on the island of Otrera, surrounded by women. We shared stories, little excerpts of the happier times before our own follies brought about the deaths of our closest companions. Even as my knees began to ache from sitting on the sand, and I could see Achilles rubbing his tired eyes, we sat together, mixing our histories together like two rivers pouring into the sea. The moon drifted lazily across the blanket of night until it drooped between the Myrmidon tents.

Then we rose without speaking. Achilles handed me up my cape, which I wrapped around myself to cover the distinctive leopard skin and cut of my armor. He nodded to me and led me around to the entrance of his tent. The sun would not rise for some hours yet, but I could see old King Priam emerging with fog in his eyes. He blinked but did not seem too surprised to find me there and not coming to blows with once-hated Achilles.

Achilles and Briseis cleared some of the ransom from Priam's cart, though Achilles brushed at it with little concern as if he was clearing dust from a long-ignored shelf. Then the Argive placed Hector's wrapped body on the cart and nodded to Priam. The old man had recovered some of his dignity throughout the night and stood again like a king at the head of the cart. I motioned that I would join him and stepped to Achilles.

"Are you still for Ilium?" he asked, running a hand over the stubble on his chin.

I nodded. "And you for the Argives?"

"Then we will be enemies when we meet on the field," he replied.

I sighed, though I felt no more regrets. "Yes, enemies. But I will do you no dishonor, Achilles."

"And I none to you."

We clasped hands as warriors, as equals.

I turned to join Priam when his voice made me look over my shoulder.

"Maybe you will see your Hippolyta soon."

"And maybe you will see your Patroclus."

We nodded to one another, and then I took up the cart with Priam, and we brought Hector's body back to Ilium.

Chapter 14 - νομάς

NOMAD

Had I known then what destruction Theseus would fashion in our lives, I would have slit his throat and let him die on my mother's stoop. But I did not, and we bowed to him with deference—but still as equals in the hierarchy of royals and common people. We were the daughters of the Queen of the Amazons, after all.

King Theseus inclined his head towards us. "It is an honor to meet the daughters of Queen Otrera," he said in his deep, throaty voice. He was handsome enough, I supposed, though his charms were lost on Otrera and myself. Hippolyta beamed back at him with her winningest smile. I was at once struck by her beauty, how soft and curved she had grown, while I stood solid as a stone column. We could both break a man's arm with no more than a flick of the wrist, but Lyta and I were no longer identical in our youthful ranginess.

Theseus was continuing, "Of course, your queen has offered me all the hospitality your island has to offer, but I see I made my visit just at the right time to meet the two of you. I have heard of you both, of course—your prowess as warriors from Ilium and from my dear friend and companion,

Heracles."

The mention of Hippolyta's former lover chilled my heart. Otrera, not knowing of his personage, simply smiled. But Lyta, dear Lyta, practically bounded forward with excitement. "You know Heracles?" she exclaimed.

The King of Athens let out a demure chuckle and nodded. "Heracles and I went on many adventures as youths. He told me of your island and how you allow only women upon it and that your women stand in for warriors, where other lands use their men." His eyes flickered across Hippolyta's face and body, though only I seemed to notice the look. "He had many praises to sing of the Amazons on Themyscira."

At that moment, Otrera moaned and reached to clutch at her ankle. She could barely touch as low as her knee, and she sank weekly into her couch, eyes pressed shut. Lyta and I rushed to her side at once.

"King Theseus," I said in a voice like stone, "let us see to our mother's ailments privately. I'm sure we will meet you again during your visit here."

The king bowed low and backed towards the doorway. "Of course. I wish your mother all the best, ladies." He was gone quickly, but I still felt as if his eyes were upon me, searing through my flesh and muscle and right down to the bones and soul. I could not explain the feeling, and so I shuddered as if I'd been standing outside in a cold rain.

Hippolyta knelt beside Mother's couch with one golden hand on Otrera's forehead and the other locked with her pain-grasping fingers. "Are you all right, Mother? Did the bones not set right?"

I hovered over them both, feeling hopeless when it

came to comfort and soothing. My nature was all sharp edges and blunt words, with none of the warmth and charm of Lyta. But I took my mother's other hand.

Otrera bit her lip in pain, then sank down into the softness of her couch. "My daughters," she said in a reedy voice, "I have had a vision."

Lyta and I shared a bewildered look before settling nearer to Otrera. "What do you mean, Mother?" asked Hippolyta.

"You know I was blessed by a god once before," she said, closing her eyes in recollection or to gather strength. "Or twice before, once for each of my beautiful daughters." I felt myself stiffen, and my fingers clutched hers a little less tightly than before. This was her talk of our father, calling him the God of War. I could accept those claims when I was a child, perhaps, but now they soured against my ears. Hippolyta, I saw, smiled at Mother and glowed with pride at her words.

"Ares," whispered Lyta, the name soft as wool on her lips, "that is what they call the War God in the lands of men." She patted Mother's cheek. "And our Moon Goddess is called Artemis." She smiled at her own words. We had learned much of the outer world in Ilium, including their endless names and titles for every little thing. I had mostly ignored such words, but Hippolyta had delighted in them, the worldliness of their usage and meaning.

Otrera nodded weakly. "Well, I have been blessed again while you were with Priam. The Moon Goddess — Artemis, as men call her — she has given me an important task. I must undertake the building of a temple in her honor." She relaxed into her pillows, exhausted by her words.

"Oh, Mother, that is wonderful!" exclaimed Hippolyta.

"Where will you build it? I saw all the new buildings when we came through town. Will you need to clear some of the trees?"

I bit my lip. We had always worshiped our Moon Goddess in the peacefulness of our homes before or under the branches of our forest trees. Why would she want us to build her a temple now? To separate us and our prayers from the forest and the world around us? I could not claim to know the will of the gods, but this felt unnatural, especially here on our quiet island. How could you see the moon from inside some building?

Our mother's eyes fluttered open, and she waved a hand to halt Hippolyta's questions. "No, child. Artemis wishes her temple built elsewhere, far to the south, farther even than Ilium. I shall need your help preparing for the journey."

"A journey!" I rose abruptly from her bedside. "Mother, you can barely lie here. How do you expect to make a journey of any length? And then dedicate a temple? You should be resting. We should be finding you new healers to help you with your leg."

But Otrera was still my mother and still the queen. "I must do this, Penthesilea. It is not our place to question the will of the gods."

Hippolyta and I shared another look that our mother didn't notice.

"Leave me, now." Otrera waved us away. "I must rest."

Once Lyta and I had exited our childhood home, we strode into what had become the village agora. I was a little surprised to find the place bustling, more than twice as crowded as it had been before. More houses filled out the village, and I could see that the forest had been cleared back a bit to accommodate even more homes and buildings. This was not the same sleepy island we had left. Something about the buildings, though…they had a measure of damage to them, remnants of ash from flame or obviously rebuilt walls. What had transpired here during our stay in Ilium? And back down by the beaches, shipwrights had been working on building boats of various sizes. The sparring grounds also appeared to have grown, and a new crop of young girls trained in all manner of armed combats. Industry had changed this place. I did not hate it, but it still made the place feel foreign, unlike the dusty home of my childhood.

Hippolyta wrapped her arm around mine and twined our fingers together. "Mother seems different," she said, tugging me through the growing village and over to watch the girls practicing their fighting. "I wonder if she means to leave Themyscira to dedicate this temple to Artemis, who will take her place here?" She stared at the girls who kicked up dust with their exertions. "Do the Amazons not need a queen?"

I squeezed her hand as we had done as children. "The island has grown since we left. I feel as if I've gotten smaller, and the world around me has gotten so big."

My sister laughed. She turned and looked me up and down. "I don't think you realize how tall you've grown, Pen." She twined one of my dark curls around her golden finger. "You have the look of a queen about you, I think."

"Oh no." I shook my head. "I'm little more than a soldier. You and Mother are the queens. Lyta, look at yourself. You're beautiful and strong, every inch the queen." I glanced down at myself, at my flat chest and square waist, the way my leg muscles bunched under the hem of my chiton. I looked nothing like the lovely queens in stories. I was too tall, too thick, too muscular. My face was too plain. But Lyta, now she looked like a queen.

Lyta sighed wistfully. "Ah, but doesn't a queen need a king?"

A shudder shot up my spine, and I spun to face her. "Does our mother need a king to rule this place?" My brow furrowed. "Has she ever needed a man to help her?"

But Hippolyta did not want to argue. "She needed a man to make us," was all she would say.

We watched the younger girls spar for a bit longer until the sun drifted to the treetops, and they scattered off to their homes and their dinners and their warm, little hearths. I snuck looks at my sister, her face open and smiling to be back in our home. I felt empty, my heart, my soul, empty—I could not explain. I wanted the town to be smaller. I wanted King Theseus and whoever else had come to entreat the Queen of Themyscira to leave. I wanted to wander the forest as a child again and not hear the sounds of labor on the beaches. It hurt me that Hippolyta was so happy to return here, with all the changes and the newness of it. It hurt that my sister, my ally in life, my constant companion, was changing. Why was I still the same? Taller, yes, stronger—but otherwise, the same girl I had been. And what did it mean that I felt no desire to change and to grow as Lyta had?

But of course, I could not answer these questions, nor could I debate it with Lyta, for she looked so peaceful and content as the sun began to set. And so I would keep my pain to myself. Perhaps in the morning, we would discuss matters again.

Morning came, and further emissaries arrived on Themyscira
to beseech Queen Otrera for aid. My mother took her council
in the wide plaza that had sprung up before her home.
Hippolyta and I stood at her side while she still lay, half-
impaired, upon her couch. The emissaries, like Theseus, had
men in their companies. The sight of them on the island irked
me, though I had never quite hated them so much as the older
women after the incident years ago to find the ban completely
necessary. Surely, I thought, men and women must be able to
find some sort of harmony amongst themselves. Yet still, the
men of these delegations came from the outer world, the one
where men ruled scepter and throne over women. They did
not—could not—see us as equals. Not as Hector or Aeneas
had.

　　　The thought of Hector brought an ache to my heart,
just as I had felt one for Otrera that first night upon the ships
after leaving home for Ilium over a year ago. I missed him
dearly. He, who had been such a stolid, equitable force in the
ranks, would make a good king one day, just like his father.
I recalled Hippolyta's question from the night before about
which of us two sisters would lead the Amazons with our
mother gone. A petty feeling within me hissed that neither of
us would be as good a queen as Otrera was.

　　　Or as good as she had been.

　　　The morning entreaties passed at an interminable
pace. Both Otrera and the visitors to our island seemed
more concerned with roundabout talking and unnecessary
formalities rather than simply making their points. I ignored
most of what was said. Some minor landowners requested

the services of the trained Amazon warriors to protect this or aid in some squabble. Were we some mercenary army now to be hired out to the highest bidder? Was this our purpose, the reason Otrera had started our island community so many years ago? But, of course, I did not know that. I had always lived in the moment here — and then immersed in my training at Ilium — that I had never thought to ask my own mother why she had separated us from the rest of the world. It had just been so. I flicked away a bee that buzzed around my head. I had always supposed the Amazons were meant as an escape from the outer world, an answer — no, a rebuttal — to the rulership of men, and one that should remain separate and distinct. Perhaps that was why this audience troubled me so, as it was a direct reversal of this previous stance. But Otrera herself had welcomed such a change, another part of me argued, so it had to align in some way with her former intention. I found no comfort in these debates of the mind, though; my heart was always clearer when my head was free of such considerations, and my lungs could breathe in the open, clean air.

But Otrera was making pronouncements now about King Theseus and his party from Athens. She took Hippolyta's hand — my sister stood closer than I, I reasoned — and told the king he could stay as long as he liked on our island. He was a royal guest of our household.

I snickered, thinking of our humble home compared to the palace of Priam and the imagined majesty of the Athenian royal residence. Otrera might be queen but of a different kind of kingdom. A kingdom of the heart and soul rather than of stone and man.

Then Otrera called together all the people of Themyscira,

or at least the ones not performing necessary tasks. "My daughters," she said, speaking not just to Hippolyta and myself but to all the Amazon women, "I must share with you my most wonderful plans. The Moon Goddess spoke to me in a vision and called me to dedicate a temple in her honor. I must leave the island." She settled the flood of comments by raising her hands for quiet. "Now, some of you were not here during the winter months when we suffered an outright attack at the hands of foreign men. For this reason, I have decided that we shall seek a new home for the Amazons. This island may not remain safe to us for much longer. Men have heard tell of us and our community, and I fear that more armies may try to invade."

My whole body shook with rage. Men had attacked Themyscira! Why had Otrera waited a whole day since we arrived to inform us? Why had no word been sent immediately to us in Priam's city? I would have ridden all night, would have flown across the clouds to get here. I would never have let our home be attacked.

Mother continued. "When I leave to go south for the dedication of my new temple, I plan to divide our force of Amazons. One half of the army will travel overland with me for a time—though their real purpose will not be joining me but finding a new place we can call home. The other half of the army will remain here on Themyscira to protect the old and infirm and to take in any newcomers that may arrive during our absence. Once a new land has been found for us, the remainder will pack up and join them there."

Lyta and I were just as frozen as the rest of the gathered women. Clearly, Otrera had not discussed her plans with any of them. The foreigners, including King Theseus, looked on with bemused expressions.

"Who will lead these two forces?" came a voice from the crowd.

Otrera smiled. "That is easy," she said. "My two accomplished daughters. Penthesilea will lead the party overland in seeking out a new home. And Hippolyta will stay on the island and protect those who remain."

It was not my wish to argue with my mother, our queen, so I followed her commands with a rock in my gut and unspoken contention on my lips. The preparations for our travel were simple, at least for me, as I had very few belongings to begin with, and those I had could easily be carried by Zephyr. I took my beloved horse on a quick canter around the island the morning of our departure to take a last look at everything in case I never returned. It felt strange to think of leaving this place that had been my home for so long, especially after having only just returned. The sun glittered against the leaves of the trees and the sand of the beaches with ferocious intensity as if to remind me of its beauty always.

When Zephyr and I returned, I found Otrera waiting on the stoop, beckoning me inside with urgency. Hippolyta was nowhere in sight; her preparations were different as she was going to stay behind. Another oddity — the idea of being parted from Lyta.

"Pen," began my mother, as I helped her inside the house, "I must give you something before we leave. It is something I have wished to give you for many years." She smiled warmly and touched my cheek, a little of her old spark gleaming in her brown eyes.

We sat together by the hearth, as we had often done during my childhood. She bade me bring forward the chest containing my father's armaments.

"Remember that day so long ago, Pen?" She opened the chest and touched her fingers lightly on the contents. "When Rastor brought this armor to me? I know you and your sister have looked at it and played with it from time to time. But today, I wish to gift some of it to you. It is your birthright. You had to earn it, just as you had to earn the leopard skin."

I readjusted the pelt that hung over my shoulder. A nervous feeling in my gut reminded me of Hippolyta's golden hands giving Heracles our father's belt as a gift. Did Mother know of this? I decided it was not my place to tell her; that would be Lyta's job if she ever admitted to it.

Mother brought out the great helmet that had belonged to my father. A horsehair crest jutted from the bronze hood, and dark eyeholes stared back at me. I bit my lip. This helmet connected me to a man I had never known, yet still, my eyes grew damp as Otrera handed it to me. I'd seen no finer helmet in my life, not on the heads of Ilium's generals nor in the armor Hector had shown me would be his someday. Silently, I thanked my mother for the gift.

"Every warrior needs a blade." Next, she handed me my father's sword, sheathed in the sleekest leather and glowing in the light of the hearth fire.

Carefully, I unsheathed the weapon, saw its fine, killing edge, and watched the firelight play across it in shades of orange and gold.

"Thank you, Mother," I said, barely a whisper.

"Do not thank me, child," said Mother in a voice I barely recognized. "Thank the gods."

My parting with Hippolyta was heartfelt and sorrowful, though we shed no tears. I could have lingered in her embrace forever. What if, I suddenly thought, something happened, and I never saw her again? My flesh, my blood, my beloved sister. But neither of us spoke such things, though I could see from her eyes that the same thoughts flashed through her mind.

King Theseus bowed obsequiously to me in farewell. It did not sit well with me that he was to remain on Themyscira even after Otrera and I had gone. But he and his fellow emissaries from Athens wanted to learn about the Amazons, and Otrera had granted him her blessing.

I was beginning to fear that her blessings and favor might carry less import than I originally thought. My mother seemed to flow from her usual lucid self to a stranger obsessed with the building of this new temple. I wanted to ask her about the attack on the island that had left her injured and changed, but some part of me refused, saying she would tell me in her own time. I had no way of knowing if she would or not.

The island of my childhood sparkled green and vibrant at my back as we loaded onto the ships that would take us to the mainland. Zephyr stood calmly upon the deck, and I rested my hand on his yellow neck, gaining strength from his solidity. He would forever remind me of Hector, my strong, honest friend. I chuckled, thinking of the horsehair crest on the helmet Hector had shown me, the one he would wear when he fought in his first battle. Perhaps he and Zephyr shared more in common than their calming influences on me.

As the island grew smaller behind our ships, I refused

to turn and look upon it. Themyscira was here, I told myself, in the hearts of the women on our ship, not in the rock and sand and trees of an island. Amazons were anywhere, and we would carry our home always in our breasts.

At last, the ships spat us out in the fertile lands around the mouth of the Thermodon River. Our first camp was nearby, inland by some miles, near a grove of fruiting trees. The next day, Mother promised we would meet with horse merchants who would supply us with enough mounts for all the women in our company. I was given the honor of training the new riders, younger girls who had lived their whole lives upon the island, or older women who had never known the feel of a saddle under their seats. That evening, Otrera blessed our dreams, and only a few women remained awake to guard the relatively large camp.

From my pallet of blankets and the pillow of my satchel beneath my head, I stared up at the open sky. Stars flickered in the dark blanket of the night, and the crescent moon sent waves of silver light to rest gently upon the camp. Did the Moon Goddess bless our journey? I hoped so. Hearing the peaceful noises from the other women urged my heart to calm, and soon I slept alongside all those others, women of all ages who had vowed to follow my mother across the ends of the earth to live among only women.

Once we gained the horses, travel became much easier. I began training the women immediately in the ways of horsemanship, finding the younger, rangier girls easiest to instruct. The older women had more complaints and pains from being in the saddle for long periods of time, but the girls came to it naturally, as if they were just another limb of their horses. Otrera, of course, could not ride, and a cart was set up for her and some of our supplies to ride in. She seemed not to mind the indignity of riding with baggage and often led the group in song from her comfortable perch. Her leg did not seem to be improving, but she never complained.

I reveled in the education of the other women, a chance to show what I had learned from Anchises in Ilium and share that knowledge with the Amazons. It shocked me how much I remembered of his little teachings and how many of his habits crept into my lessons. The girls learned to ride horseback, of course, but also how to fire arrows while riding and how to aim with a spear and sword from the saddle. Usually, our days were spent riding, traveling and training, and our nights were spent camped under the stars, sharing the bonds of community and sisterhood together. Mostly the land was undulated with rocks and plains, the occasional stands of trees or farms breaking the monotony.

It was a different life than I'd led before, but I found the days refreshing and the education of the other women difficult yet satisfying. More and more, the women came to me instead of Otrera with their issues or complaints, and I liked how the honor felt on my shoulders.

So far, our travels took us far inland from the Thermodon, days south, and steadily traveling west, though not anywhere near the Hellespont or Ilium. I missed those days, the carefree young times training with Anchises, but I missed them less and less as we straggled throughout the greatness of Anatolia, following roads and paths as our whims took us. Or took me, rather, for most of the navigating was done by myself. I kept us away from most of the cities, except for when we traded for supplies in some of the smaller towns. As I took over the leadership of the group, Otrera became more of our moral guidance, the font from which history and myth sprung each night around the campfires.

Otrera spoke of gods and heroes, adventures and legends, but never of the world we knew. She did not speak of her founding of Themyscira, nor did she explain the attack on the island that had happened while Hippolyta and I were away.

So far, our travels had not brought us anywhere permanent to relocate, but the edges of the horizon became the boundaries of our yard and training ground. We hunted and rode and camped and learned. Our home was the world, and our goals were simple. I thrilled at the open sky and wide plains and the sun, always the sun, peering down on us like a gracious nanny. We hunted, and we rode, and we slept under the stars, and we rejoiced in the very act of living. As we continued to live off the land, I found myself growing farther from Otrera. She felt less like my mother and our queen than she did like a living legend herself, the mouthpiece of history and lore. I couldn't rightly say if the change hurt me. Perhaps all girls go through this with their parents, for you cannot stay a child forever. But I did not know, and there was no Hippolyta to confer with to see if she felt the same. She was queen of the island, while I was queen of riders and horses. And our mother was queen of the past.

Three queens, each with our own parts to play.

Over many months, we circled the lands around the Thermodon, wending this way and that across the bountiful landscape. If I had known what was then transpiring back on the island, I would have rounded up our entire force and thundered back north. But I had no way of telling the trouble Hippolyta would bring upon herself, and so I trusted her to rule as queen while we searched for a new home.

The coast came upon us in a glittering sea of dark-red wine at dusk one day. The women smiled and danced into the waters of the sea. Someone called out that we had finally reached the Aegean Sea, the one I recalled from my time at Ilium. Otrera rose from her cart and, with the help of some of her caretakers, staggered towards the sand. I let Zephyr frolick into the low waves before I went over and sat beside my mother.

"Here," Otrera said, letting out a deep sigh. Her eyes scanned the sunlight gleaming across the water. "This is where our temple shall go."

This was a shock. After so much time, I had almost forgotten she intended to build a temple. "Why here, Mother?" I asked. There was nothing on the gray-brown coast or the whispering waves that made this region any different from any other we'd passed through, at least not in my eyes.

Otrera refused to look at me, though she gave much attention to the women laughing and girls playing in the water. "Penthesilea, this is my vision. We must begin the temple building here. It is what Artemis wishes."

My Moon Goddess had never wanted any such thing, I thought, but I did not speak. It was hard to have my mother care so much and feel so strongly about this temple and its dedication. It meant so little to me.

"When you were gone, I told you that men attacked us." She fell silent though her voice had not shaken with torment at the memory. I held my breath, willing her to continue.

She sighed and spoke again after a long moment. "The

men flooded the beaches. They stormed our very homes." I
nodded. I had seen the damage left from the attack. "It was
during the invasion that my leg was broken. I fought against
so many, but some men caught me and fractured my body.
But we protected ourselves, Pen. It was only with the strength
of Artemis that we were able to fight them back to the beaches,
back to their ships."

I clenched my jaw. More likely that the women's own
strength and training had pushed back the fighters. Why did
my mother insist so heavily on this?

"That is why," she went on, "we must build this temple
in her honor. I have seen the future. The temple will be a great
place to her worship. It will give girls and women strength,
just as Artemis gave us strength in those moments."

"But why build it here?" I asked at last. "Why not back
on our island?"

Otrera shook her head. "You would not understand,
Pen. The goddess has not blessed you with her vision."

She was right. I did not understand. Nor did I want to.
Our people had good lives back home, and we had learned
a new way of life traversing the lands on horseback. Why
stop and build a temple so far from home? And why had we
not avenged the attack on our island? Why allow those men
to escape the ire of our vengeance? It was well within our
power and our duty to do so. Yet here was our queen, my
own mother, focusing all her energies on building a temple
when we could have been protecting ourselves from another
such incident.

But there was no arguing with my mother; though I
had taken the reins in many ways, she was still one of our
queens. A small contingent of women were selected to design

and build the temple. My mother chose them each by hand, described her vision to them, and then joined the rest of our troop in our continued travels around Anatolia. Occasionally we would revisit the temple's planned spot on the coast, but with little for us to do besides get in the way, we often turned back to our travels.

Almost a year had gone by, and my women and I had become almost fully nomadic. We could strike camp and ride with only a moment's notice, and even the old maids could sling with good aim from horseback. Mother still hadn't recovered, but I was busy with the ruling of the group and so had let such concerns fade with time.

But not all concerns could disappear.

One evening, a messenger found us camped at the base of a low bluff. Otrera and another woman were singing praises to the Moon Goddess before the fire when the young girl staggered into our camp, her face drawn from exertion and her limbs shaking. We gave her food and drink before she was able to share her news.

"There is trouble on Themyscira, my queen," she choked out. It was unclear if she meant me or Otrera.

"What has happened?" I asked, my hand going to my father's sword, though clearly there was no immediate threat such as would need a blade.

"Queen Hippolyta has left Themyscira, my lady," explained the messenger. We sat around her, stunned, not understanding. "She has gone to Athens with King Theseus."

"Why would she go to Athens?" I asked at last. The other women wore troubled looks and exchanged glances with each other, faces blue in the drooping sunlight.

"She went to Athens as the wife of King Theseus, my

queen."

Chapter 15 - πόλεμος

THE WAR

Fresh clarity woke me the morning of my final duel with Achilles. It soothed my sore muscles like a balm, relieved the pain in my head, and eased my nerves. I was stillness and calm. I was a breath of the air, a flower tugged gently in a soft wind. No more did doubt tear at my mind. I was Penthesilea. I was the Queen of the Amazons.

And I might die this day.

The prospect of death did not loom over me with terror any longer, but neither did it pull to me through my desperation and sadness. I sucked in a deep breath and rose from my bed. After returning to Ilium with Priam, I had only slept a short time, perhaps only minutes. But I did not care. What need had a dying body for sleep? What more cause for rest could I have in the face of death?

I stood before my armor, where I had laid it all out across a table in my chamber. There was the familiar helmet, its red horsehair crest going a little ragged since the days of my father. There were the bronze greaves that had saved my legs from being mangled in more than one battle. I drew my fingers along the length of my sword hilt, feeling little dings and nicks that had accumulated in the leather over time. These, the breastplate of woven plates, the metal cuffs, and my leopard pelt—all as familiar to me as my own skin. I sighed. This might be the last time I wore them, the last time I girded myself like this and strode into battle.

A sound at my door. I turned to see it creak open. A tanned face peered at me through the crack. Polemusa, one of my Amazon warriors. She and all the others had trained here with me when we were younger. It was like looking into the past—at a happier past—to see them crowding the doorway like fresh girls, spilling over with untold secrets.

I beckoned them into my rooms.

On bare feet, they padded in, forming a circle around me.

It was Klonie who spoke first, a woman with deeply tanned skin and vivid red curls.

"My queen, we are here to see if you will ride with Ilium again," she said. Her voice was harsh and raspy from a wound she'd sustained to her neck years ago.

I bowed my head and took the time to look each warrior in the face before I spoke. I recalled my sister, praising them each by name that first night we came to Ilium so many years ago.

"I ride for Ilium today, yes," I said at last. "But I cannot ask you to do the same. You do not have the same burden of guilt that I have. You do not have the shame of Queen Hippolyta's blood on your hands. You need to atone for nothing."

Klonie shook her head, as did the others. "We are not here to atone for anything. We are friends of Ilium. We trained here, just as you did. This is our home as well as yours."

Evandre spoke up. "We will die here to protect our friends."

I remembered that Evandre had been especially close to Axion, a son of Priam, during our earlier time in the city. Axion, a boy with fair hair and kind eyes. Axion, a son of Ilium, dead at the hands of the Argives.

Polemusa took my hand in hers. "We have all lost those we love, Penthesilea. We want to fight today."

I bit my lip and shook my head. "The Argives far outnumber us. I see now that Ilium may fall." I looked at the Amazons. Dry eyes all around. "We will likely die today." I had resigned myself to this fact, but they did not have to share my fate.

Together, they closed their circle, hands touching each other, touching me. Warmth and electricity surged through us all like a lightning bolt in a storm cloud.

"We will fight at your side," whispered Evandre. "We know what it means to honor those we love. And those we have lost."

Together, my women and I armed ourselves. We took turns helping each other, lacing up armor, buckling hard to reach spots, girding ourselves for war. There was silence, but it was a comforting silence. It allowed us each to consider our paths, maybe to ponder our pasts, as I was doing.

Hector had spoken to me about fate when he bemoaned wedding a girl he didn't know. And Achilles had talked of it the previous night—fate, a thread that tied together all your actions, past and future, and pressed you into the proper direction. I did not like the idea of being burdened by fate, by a power I could not control. I'd had enough of following threads of fate like a dog on a leash. I wanted to make my own choices. I wanted to create my own path.

I settled the familiar leopard pelt on my shoulders. Rather more tattered than it had been in my childhood, I found its weight and warmth comforting. So much like the old times. And yet perhaps the end. Or the start of something new.

When we emerged from within and made our way to the stables where our horses were kept, I was surprised to see an old friend standing beside Zephyr. Aeneas, his blonde hair darkened with age and his skin as tan as a hickory nut, patted my horse's cheek with one hand, the other resting lazily on the hilt of his sword.

"Aeneas, old friend," I called in greeting.

He patted Zephyr once more and turned to us. Most of the women, remembering him, waved or nodded. He smiled back. Apparently, in the passing years, he'd shed his shyness and blossomed into a real man, one that legends might later call a hero.

"My queen," he said, sweeping into a dramatic bow.

I grinned at him. "None of that, Aeneas."

He straightened. "I'm to lead the charge today," he said. "You all look armed. Does this mean we can count on your support in the fight?"

Nodded, I tightened my belt, though it needed no adjustment. "Aye, prince. We ride for Ilium, and we will ride for it as long as we hold breath in our bodies and life in our bones."

Aeneas looked proud then, proud of his people, proud of their heroic stand, while Death pounded on the Skaian

Gates, proud to call us strange warrior-women friends. "I hope we all have long lives ahead of us, Penthesilea. Not just me, but your Amazons too."

"As do I," I concurred quietly, "yet the gods may have other plans for us."

Fate, always fate. For without fate, would I have met Hector? Would I have saved Lyta from the leopard? Would any event, no matter how sorry or sad, have happened the way it did? I did not know. And perhaps I did not care. It was for better men or women than me to philosophize about such things. I was a warrior. I carried guilt. I would atone here on the sands before Ilium. And I had a higher purpose— to defend Ilium down to its last man. Maybe that was my fate. To defend Priam's city.

I spat on the ground before our horses. What did I care about fate? I was doing my duty. I was following my beliefs. I was doing what I thought was right. Fate could fuck off.

Aeneas and I clasped hands as men did. "Ilium is lucky to have you at its side, Penthesilea. You and all your Amazons."

"And we are lucky to have friends like you, Aeneas."

Another figure approached before I could mount Zephyr. Be-ringed and decked in sumptuous robes, my least favorite son of Priam drew near. Paris. My lip curled a little at the sight of his fiery curls and handsome features. He must have seen the look on my face because he shook his head and splayed his hands in deference.

I glared down my nose at him as he stooped before me.

"What do you want?" The earlier clearness of my brain seemed to fog at his approach.

Paris chewed his lower lip, refusing to look me in the

eyes before dropping to the ground before me. The knees of his robes sank in the dust and dirt. All stubbornness and condescension smoothed from his face.

"I saw Hector," he said, his voice low, barely heard over the horses and their harnesses and the Amazon women preparing their gear.

I stared at him without speaking.

"What you've done," he sputtered, "what you helped my father do—"

"Are you thanking me, son of Priam?" I said, my words cutting like metal.

A flash of his old animosity sparked behind his eyes, but Paris choked it down. "I know I have spoken...not well with you before. But I know you loved Hector in your way. It was a good thing you've done for my father. And for Ilium."

My hand clenched around my sword hilt. "We all fight for Ilium. My women and all these men from your city. We all do good for Ilium." I paused. "You could too." I recalled him during our training with Anchises. He had been annoying but not a terrible fighter.

Paris' head sank in shame. "I cannot fight. I want to, but I cannot." He looked up at me then, his eyes red and watery. "I know that I must, but my heart rebels. I am . . . I am not as brave as you are, Penthesilea."

The fact that Paris finally acknowledged my prowess and the courage of the other Amazons pried its way into my heart. I saw him for what he was, a spoiled boy, tossed into a world that gave him all, then took back whatever it wanted — churned on the waves of fate just as much as I was or Achilles or Hippolyta. I did not pity him, for he was still the boy who insulted and threatened me and spoke ill of my friends. But

I saw the threads of his fate, at once dangling over the flame of death as it entwined with the thread of Helen's life as well. So were we all connected by fate, connected to it, controlled, nay, enslaved by it.

"We choose who we are, Paris," I said. "I choose to stand before the gates of Ilium and raise my sword. What you call bravery is just another choice."

Paris looked away.

"That is where I choose to be now." I turned and strode to Zephyr and my women.

We mounted and rode with the other troops towards the gates. The ragged people of Ilium gathered about their windows and street corners and rooftops to watch the procession. Priam, like always, stood with Hecuba and Andromache above the gatehouse on the walls where he could see the fighting. He willed himself each day to watch every spear thrust, to see each man of Ilium fall dead to the earth. He looked a little braver this morning, stood a little taller, the color in his face a little deeper. The women stood on either side of him, hands clasped with his. They all looked stronger now that Hector's body had been returned. Helen was with them, without her weasel of a husband. Her back was straight, and she stared out at the battlefield like a goddess not of beauty but of war.

Good, I thought. This was the beginning of putting things to right for both sides of the war. I thought of Achilles, seated behind his tent, staring up at the moon with me, mourning his dear Patroclus. He and I were the same, two sides of the same coin, worth little in the grand marketplace of the world. But here we were. Warriors. And we would do what we did best.

The Skaian Gates creaked open. How many times had they done so in the course of this war? Out we rode, the host of Ilium, resplendent in armor and glory. So many chariots, so many horses, so many warriors and foot soldiers. But only thirteen women.

The Argive host spilled from their camp, dark-armored warriors leading their charge. I recognized the Myrmidons even before their chariots rumbled over the dying river Scamander that separated our forces. I smiled. Achilles would be there at the head of the assault.

I set my jaw with determination. Despite our conversation, I still planned to fight him, as he planned to try and slay me. We had made our promises to our kings. We knew we were pawns in this larger game. But we would play our parts with honor this time.

Before the two armies collided, a weird peace fell over us. There was the creak of leather, the crack of arrows in quivers, the deep breaths of men running and horses straining from both sides. I sucked in a deep breath and picked out a target among the Argives. I tightened my grip on my spear.

The two sides crashed together like tidal waves, meshing men and horses and chariots almost immediately. My spear tore into the first man I'd targeted, and he fell screaming from the back of his chariot. His driver turned around in shock, inadvertently colliding with the iron wheels of some man of Ilium. Both chariots went down. All around me, men on both sides of the fight wailed and died and killed. Horses rose on their rear legs and smashed the skulls of men around them when they dropped back down onto four hooves. I steered Zephyr through the bloody press of people. We dodged spear thrusts and sword slashes while dealing a fair number of our own.

How fared my women? Through the blood spattered on me, I stared at the battlefield. Nearby, Klonie was stabbing a man through his neck, roaring a warcry that could be heard back in Athens. Before she could yank back her spear, a hooked weapon jutted forwards and tore into her breastplate. The man wielding it yanked back on his pike, drawing forth the contents of Klonie's belly. Blood spurted from her lips, and she keeled backwards over the seat of her gray horse.

"No!" I screamed. Klonie, a dear girl, a friend, a sister. The first of us to die. I swung my sword down and ripped through the soft leather armor coating her killer's arm, which fell from his body, severed like a twig of wood onto the bloody sand. I did not stay to watch him die, but die he would, for he could not survive such a wound.

I killed another man and another. But they killed my allies. I saw two sons of Priam fall together at the hands of some Argive hero, a man so tall and wide, I would have sworn him to be a giant. Evandre, on some borrowed horse after hers had died the day before, took an arrow through the eyehole of her helm and dropped from the saddle. Two other Amazons, too far from me across the battlefield to recognize, were taken down by hordes of circling charioteers. I raised my shield just in time for an arrow to sink into it. The sharp point looked like a little leaf that pierced my shield and bit into the skin of my forearm. Blood coursed from the wound. I took a deep breath and ignored the pain.

Another Amazon fell, Bremusa with her dark, flashing eyes, crushed under the weight of her horse as he screamed on the ground, his side punctured by so many spearpoints.

I swore and slew another Argive and another. Where

was Achilles? Only his death, or mine, could stop this mayhem.

There! A dark flash as the sunlight glinted off pure black armor. Achilles turned his helmet to me. The shadows cast by the nose and cheek guards hid his face from view. In the sunlight, I imagined my tattered leopard pelt hanging over his right shoulder. We were the same, he and I, I thought again.

I kicked my heels into Zephyr and galloped across the battlefield to face myself.

Chapter 16 - θάνατος

DEATH

I was for riding back to Themyscira, but Otrera, in one of her final moments acting as Queen of the Amazons, ordered us to stay at camp by the bluff until morning. A few of the other women felt as I did, I could tell, but none argued with my mother. I spent the night restlessly, wandering the camp or lying in my bedroll, staring up at the sky, begging the moon for an answer. None came. Why would Hippolyta abandon Themyscira? Why would she leave the Amazons back on the island without a queen? Could she truly love this man, this King of Athens?

When we broke camp, again Otrera argued with me. She refused to ride north with us, claiming she had to return to the growing temple. I raged at her, though she was my mother — she had changed from the mother I knew.

"Why have we ridden for almost a year with so few stops to build your temple to the Moon Goddess?" I asked. "Why must you return to it now, of all times?"

Otrera shook her head. "Artemis has spoken. I will not return to Themyscira with you. But you may go if you like. But, daughter," clarity appeared briefly in her eyes, "you may regret what you do now, what events are being set in motion."

But I would not listen. Some of the others stayed with Otrera, but the warriors who had trained with me at Ilium and most of our company saddled their horses and plunged north. This time there was no meandering path across the plains, no wandering this way and that across the highlands. Once, early one morning, while we broke camp, a group of men rode on us, weapons drawn. They thought they had come across a band of women, weak and easy for plundering and worse.

Those men's heads reclined on some grassy knoll, their gaping mouths catching rainfall until the vultures and other scavengers found them. I led the charge against any attackers, inspiring fear in any men who tried to hurt us. It was then that we became an army, not just well-trained, but experienced with battles too.

For many days we rode north towards the Thermodon. I hadn't realized how far we'd gotten in our travels. Had we passed within a spear throw of Ilium? But visiting Hector and Aeneas and Priam was not my concern now. We huddled under the leaves of a small grove of trees as rains pounded down upon us, like reminders by the gods that they still existed and still held power over us. I wrapped my leopard skin tighter around me. Would that Hippolyta were here, I thought ruefully. She would have made such a storm into a magical event. Or even my mother, or my mother as I had known her during my childhood, not this confused, worshiping creature she had become. I craved the comfort of a family that no longer existed. The memory of us three, tucked in blankets and seated before our little hearth, brought a smile to my face.

One of the warrior women who'd trained at Ilium, Antibrote, brought me over a jug of wine to share with her. She'd traded for it before our mad ride north. We huddled close under the leaves and our horse blankets.

"Why would Hippolyta take Theseus as her husband?" I wondered out loud.

Antibrote shrugged and took a swig of the wine, which was very sweet, like her rounded cheeks. "Perhaps she loves him." She rubbed the back of her hand against her chin. "Or she thinks she does."

I chewed my lip. "Have you ever wanted a husband?" I asked her. None of us Amazons had husbands, though I knew more than a few had bonded with the boys back in Ilium.

"Why would I need a husband?" Antibrote countered. "I am wife to the whole world, married to my freedom." She looked me in the eyes and took my hand in her free one. "What other women can say the same?"

I squeezed her hand. Bright Antibrote had a point. I needed no husband nor a wife. I was my own. I belonged to no man.

We arrived at our island just as dusk settled over it. Antandre, one of the warriors from Ilium who had stayed with the islanders to protect them, met us on the beach after being ferried over on those new ships. She held a lantern in one hand and a scowl on her face as she led us deeper into the city. Faces peered at us from the windows and doorways of the homes.

"Was she taken by force, Antandre?" I asked once our little group of warriors convened in the home that had once been mine and Otrera's.

Antandre shook her head. "No, my queen. She went with Theseus willingly." She bowed her head as if trying to keep me from seeing whatever expression had formed on her face.

"What is it?"

The woman looked up, and I saw her face was marred with confusion and pain. "My queen, your sister—she was, that is, she is carrying Theseus' child."

I almost reeled back into the wall at her words. "What?" She had to be lying.

"Queen Hippolyta was heavily pregnant when she left here with the King of Athens." Antandre bowed her head as if my sister's shame was her own.

I bowed my head as well, in rage instead of shame, and the other women were silent. All I heard was the buzzing of my own anger in my ears.

Did Hippolyta love this man more than she loved us that she would leave with him? Did she care more about having a child than she did about being our queen? Angry tears burned in the corners of my eyes. I simply could not understand her desire to be loved by men or her desire to carry a child. They were not my desires. My body revolted at the thought. But she had left her entire world behind for this. Why?

Finally, I cleared my throat, and the other Amazons peered up at me with deference. "We go to Athens," I said, my voice flat and devoid of any anger or discomposure.

"Are we going to war?" came one woman's voice, Derinoe, I thought.

"That is yet to be seen," I said. "But we must be ready

for it."

Our ships glided through the Bosporus strait like bone needles being threaded on the first try. We women were silent. No raucous sea shanties, no sailor stories. We had learned a little of sea travel from Ilium, and what we didn't know, we made up for in overconfidence. I stood at the prow of one of our ships like a carven figurehead, unmoving, even as the wind blustered around me and blew my cloak and hair up wildly. I felt as if I could see Hippolyta before me, standing on the sands of some foreign shore, her belly heavy with child.

"Why did you leave me?" I wanted to ask. "Why did you leave us?"

But my vision-Hippolyta could not answer. She was nothing more than dreams and wishes. Would I even find her alive in Athens? I could hope but hope only went so far. A shiver ran through me, recalling the death of that poor girl so many years ago, who had borne a disfigured child that caused those men to attack.

One day, we sailed nearer to the shore, and men from the coast yelled and screamed and tried to attack. The warrior Antibrote cast a spear from the deck of our second ship. The spear killed a man instantly, and the others fell back and stared at us blankly as we floated by. I smiled my thanks at Antibrote. In the gloomy morning, she looked almost as tall and dark as me. After that, all of us kept our weapons close at hand in case some other marauders took umbrage at the sight of unescorted women on their waters.

Once we passed through the Hellespont, we entered the Aegean Sea. Balmy breezes filled our sails and ruffled our hair. Athens was nearby. I could practically smell the oils King Theseus curled into his hair and beard. I had to know if my sister loved him, if she really wanted to be with him in Athens—or if he had taken her there against her will. Living among women outcast or fled from society, I understood the myriad depths men plumbed when they wished to love a woman, not all of them involving the woman's compliance. Had such horrors been wreaked upon my Lyta? Had Theseus taken her by force, first physically, then compelled her to join him in Athens? The sour looks of the warriors around me told me they asked themselves the same question. I was afraid to see my Lyta then—for could my heart stand to see my sister broken, body and mind? I had already hardened my heart against the bizarre changes in my mother. I did not know if I could suffer any more pain.

As we closed on Argive waters, more and more ships passed us by. Sailors stared from the decks, wondering what had brought the Amazons from their plains and hills to the waters of men. Always we scudded on peacefully, though not all the looks we received were friendly. Never to fit into this society, I supposed, my hands gripping the wooden balustrade as we neared a rocky island. Fishermen peered at us from their little coracles. There was a place for men in the world and a place for women, but not a place for Amazons.

Tensions ran high as we sailed into the harbor at Piraeus. The city of Athens had been built not on the coast but further inland, and Piraeus acted as a vassal limb that hunkered by the sea. Our path took us around the rounded nub of hilly land and into the protected harbor. A major port of call for merchants and travelers, many berths at the harborage were filled, but upon seeing us, a dock opened quickly.

Stone buildings painted in garish reds, blues, and yellows loomed over the entire harbor. So much red paint, looking like blood, staining the temples and official buildings. I rode Zephyr through the town with my women similarly astride their own mounts. Quiet stares met us as we clopped through Piraeus and headed along the Piraean Road that led northeast into Athens proper. Nothing but low greenery lined the northeastern road. The world seemed to have stilled somehow, paused itself because of our procession, and I felt like I was making my way to my own funeral pyre.

One of the other women's horses nickered nervously as we approached the walled city of Athens. It reminded me of Ilium, though not quite as grand — probably because of my preference for Priam and his city and not any fault of Athens itself. A gatehouse rose from the wall beside the entrance to the city, the gate standing open to any travelers and traders. From inside the walls, I could just make out several hills that jutted up from the homes and warehouses and other buildings. Grand temples perched atop the largest hill, every painted stone gleaming in the yellow sunlight.

Once the men at the gatehouse took note of our presence and realized why we stood upon their doorstep, a large contingent of armed men escorted us with relative peace to the home of Theseus. The king lived in a massive stone palace that impressed me very little. What did men hide from the eyes of the gods in their stone prisons? Servants and sycophants lurked and scurried everywhere. We met the king in his receiving room and found him seated on a couch draped in purple fabric and pillows.

His rosy cheeks lifted in a smile, and he looked genuinely pleased to see us. I tightened my hands into fists.

"Ah, my dearest Queen Penthesilea," he exclaimed, rising from his chair and striding towards us, his sandals slapping softly against the stone floor. "I am eager to welcome you to Athens. It has been, what, over a year since I bid you farewell from Themyscira?"

At the mention of our island's name, some of the women at my back made to step forward, hands on their weapons. I stopped them with a small motion of my hand.

"Where is my sister, King Theseus?" I asked through gritted teeth.

The king's smile widened. "Ah, but of course." He slid back to his throne and waved a beringed hand at some servant. "Fetch my lovely wife, won't you?"

I bridled at the use of the term 'wife' but otherwise held my composure. Oh gods, I prayed, which I rarely did. Please let Lyta be unharmed.

And then Hippolyta was sweeping into the chamber. Her unbound hair floated in a mass of curls behind her strong shoulders. She smiled and picked up the skirt of her long, purple gown to more quickly rush into my arms.

I hugged her more tightly than I had thought possible, wanting nothing more than to feel her body alive and well in my arms, to impress the knowledge of her safety on my heart and mind.

"Lyta, dearest," I whispered into her sweet-smelling curls, "are you safe here, unhurt?"

Sparkling laughter escaped her lips as she pulled back from my grasp. "Of course, sister!" she replied. "I have never been happier."

I thought of the times we spent together and with Mother during our childhoods and the times in Ilium, smiling and laughing—and winced at her words.

"But you left the island so suddenly," I argued. "There was a messenger who came to search for us. Why did you leave the post Mother gave you?"

Hippolyta smiled up at me, though somehow still made me feel like the silly little sister. "You are so worried about me, sister, but if I were in danger, why is Otrera not here? Surely, if there were a threat, she would have led the charge. I fear you and your Amazons have come here for the wrong reasons."

Your Amazons.

The words hung in the air like heavy clouds. No weak wind could disperse them.

So Hippolyta no longer thought of herself as one of us Amazons.

"Come, sister," she said, taking my hand as if she had not just broken my whole heart, "come and meet my son."

I took a moment to compress my shattered feelings and fuse them into some semblance of strength before I could follow her. A servant entered through a side door, her hands overflowing with a babe wrapped in rich swaddling. My Amazons—Hippolyta's friends—flowed around us. Hippolyta took the baby from the servant's hands and squeezed him against her breast.

"Here he is," she cooed into the squished, red little face. "Here is my Hippolytus."

I stared down at the little figure in her arms. He looked nothing like my sister nor Theseus, but only vaguely human, in the way most newborn infants do. I stared at him and felt only resentment in my breast, a dishonorable feeling, I knew. I felt my jaw quiver and bit down on my tongue to compose myself. How dearly Lyta held the child, how caring she looked, how like a mother.

I could never do that. I could never hold an infant and not cause it fear. I was all hard angles and armor, none of the soft, feminine warmth of Lyta and all other mothers the world over. I wanted to scream, to cry, to shed tears for the motherhood I would never embrace nor even desire. This disgust I felt for the child was disgust for myself. How could Lyta, raised just the same as me, how could she fit the mold of motherhood and womanhood, and I could not? What was wrong with me that I desired no such thing—that I, in fact, was almost sickened by it?

All these thoughts filled my head and threatened to spill in torrents from my lips. But I held my tongue, and one by one, the Amazons greeted Hippolyta's little son like he was a noble warrior. Maybe someday he would be one. Or maybe he would be a poet, or a king, like his father.

I would never know.

Theseus offered us boarding in his palace, but I refused. Instead, I argued that my women and I would sleep under the open sky on one of the hills within the city limits of Athens. It was called the Areopagus. The hill of Ares. Little stood atop the rocky slope, and I wanted to be close to the sky, as far from the choking, cramped quarters of the city.

"Please, you are my guests," countered King Theseus. He could not stand to look a fool before his own citizens.

"I am the daughter of Ares," I said, invoking the ridiculous legend Otrera had spun, "and I wish to sleep on the hill of my father."

And so we camped on the hill of Ares that night and for a few nights until, predictably, the final tragedy revealed itself.

Our days were spent uneasily in the city of Athens, buying and bartering whatever we needed for what had seemed to become a lengthy stay. The Athenians welcomed us at arm's length. What were we? Women? Men? Something else entirely? They did not understand. Maybe none of us did. We Amazons had only lived the one way, yet the world seemed not to accept what, to us, came naturally. Our nights, we camped and guarded our position on the hill, quietly fortifying our position in case we became threatened.

It was not a band of warriors or thieves or murderers that came to us in the night. No, it was my sister.

Hippolyta, face streaked with tears and dirt, hair unbrushed, and gown askew, raced up the little path to our camp one day after the sun had set. Stars and campfires and a rounding moon lit her way, and everyone stepped back when ragged and desperate, she exploded into the heart of our camp. Her bare feet looked torn and bloody from running. Dark circles presented themselves under her tear-filled eyes. She sank onto the stony ground and dug her hands into her hair.

I raced over from my tent and grabbed her shoulders in my calloused hands. "What has he done to you?" I demanded.

For a time, she could not talk, only whimper like an animal in pain. I had never seen my sister struck so low. I could hardly breathe with fear and anger.

"He took my son," she said at last, her voice hitching with tears. "He took him from my arms. Oh, Pen, he says he doesn't want me. He says he has found a new wife." She wept openly. The other Amazons stood like statues around us. "He took my Hippolytus."

I threw my arms around her and hugged her tight. Gods, she felt like a little old toy, ready to break apart from use.

"I'm so sorry, Lyta," I whispered. "I'm sorry." My voice rose as I released her so she could see the determination and hatred in my eyes. "Lyta, we can still stop him. We can get your son back."

Lyta nodded her head, though her eyes were blank and without understanding.

"We can wage war on Theseus."

I wish to all the gods and daimones and monsters of the world that I had never spoken those words. But they were said, and the Amazons made ready for war.

Before much time had passed, Theseus apparently sent a troop of Athenian soldiers to escort us from the Areopagus, but we were waiting for them. We slew a number of men with javelins, then rode our horses around the remainder, driving them down the hill and back into their city. An uneasy truce came that morning when a messenger arrived under an olive branch born in shaky hands.

"King Theseus requests you leave the city peacefully," intoned the messenger from halfway down the hill. His quaking knees refused to join us at the hill's crown. "He will give you safe passage down to Piraeus and asks you not return to Athens."

I looked at Hippolyta. She held a dark cloak about herself and stared off into some middle distance.

"We want the infant that belongs to my sister," I said. My voice rang clear. "We want her son Hippolytus. Only then will we leave."

The messenger switched the olive branch from one sweaty, shaking hand to the other. "The king will not be parted from his son."

"Then he will be parted with his life."

From our supplies, we managed to collect enough extra armor to outfit Hippolyta as an Amazon warrior and no longer the wife of King Theseus. When I offered her the panoply, she only shook her head and turned away.

"Lyta, what if we must fight our way out of here?" I asked. "Would you go unprotected?"

She refused to meet my gaze. "I have no wish to fight. I only want Hippolytus."

And so we planned our attack. Several more assaults on the hilltop occurred, but none succeeded in storming our camp. No matter how many warriors Athens threw at us, we held the hill. Maybe we were the daughters of Ares, I thought ruefully and destined to hold the hill in our father's name.

The full moon rose one day a little before dusk. Our Artemis filled Athens with her soft, silver light. A parade threaded its way through the streets of the city below as if a force of warriors did not hold one of their holy hills. Well, maybe fourteen women did not seem too much of a threat to Theseus. To the men he'd sent against us, to the men we killed, yes. But not to the king.

It was his wedding procession. Celebrants sang and danced through the streets. Lanterns lit the way to his palace.

This was the final insult. I saw Hippolyta watching the procession, tears falling down her cheeks.

Rage or divine influence filled me. I was armed and sitting astride Zephyr before I knew it. The other Amazons followed my lead as if I had commanded them thus, and struck our camp instantly. We all knew we wouldn't be returning. We thundered down the hill like an army of wraiths, cloaks and capes flapping in the wind we ourselves stirred up.

The men assigned to guard the base of the Areopagus stood little chance against us. From the high ground, we were able to let loose arrows and spears with greater accuracy, and, as the attackers, we held the element of surprise in our palms. The guards fell to a man, though they showed remarkable heroism by not retreating.

Warriors between us and the home of Theseus fell before our hooves. The roads ran red with their blood. We did not rampage through the city, though. We only wanted Theseus.

I cared only to see him dead for what he'd done to Lyta.

My sister rode behind me on Zephyr, her arms circling my waist like another cuirass. Wind whistled against my bare arms. I felt like one of the Erinyes, cloaked in vengeance. Hippolyta was silent.

Klonie fired arrows into the bodies of the guards outside Theseus' home. They dropped on the stone steps like fallen trees. We ignored them and barrelled up the steps, still on horseback. I kicked Zephyr's flanks, and he reared up, lashing his hooves against the door and sending bits of wood and debris flying.

We were inside the palace and dismounting, drawing our swords and bellowing war cries before the household knew what had descended upon them. Wedding guests screamed in terror. Servants pelted for the exits. Theseus and some young trollop, holding each other intimately at the other end of the room, turned to us and blanched.

Then Theseus, a renowned hero and warrior in his own youth, recalled himself and shouted for the guards.

Armed men appeared from nowhere, spilling food and ceremonial nuts and fruits onto the floor in their rush to attack. The Amazons fanned out against the newcomers. We tore and slashed, injuring and killing. I cared not which. I thrust my sword almost absently into the belly of some unknown man, my eyes tracking Theseus as he left his new bride and reached for a sword that hung from one wall. He stared back at me, the coldness and malevolence I had always suspected from him in full view in his eyes. Yes, he looked every inch the heroic man, garbed in dishonor and lies.

I had to tangle my way through one or two more guardsmen before I found myself standing before Theseus. He parried my first blow with his massive bronze sword, then laughed in my face.

"You think you and your women can take Athens?" he scoffed. He swung low with his sword, but I deflected it easily.

"We don't want Athens," I said with a grimace. "We only want Hippolytus."

"The boy is mine!" Fury flamed in his eyes, and his blows became wilder, harder to track and predict. He was like a wild animal trapped in the guise of a man. All the more reason to kill him where he stood.

"The boy belongs to no man!" I cried. With a booted foot, I kicked his wrist, causing him to drop his sword. With my helmet, I butted his head. A crack resounded, and he fell to his knees. I flipped my grip on my own blade and raised it over my head, preparing to bury it in his lying breast.

"No!" came a cry. It sounded both too far and too close to me as I brought down my sword. A figure blurred in front of Theseus, a dark shape interrupting my blow.

My death blow. The strike aimed at Theseus' heart.

The blow instead tore through Hippolyta's sobbing breast.

Blood pounded in my head just as it spread from her wound and coated my hands.

Lyta.

My Lyta.

Dead, at my hands. My sword, gods, our father's sword piercing her soft skin.

I turned my eyes from her glazed eyes to the shocked face of Theseus and screamed.

Chapter 17 - πόλεμος

THE WAR

Men had poured from their chariots and threw themselves into the jumbled press of warring bodies. Some hand grabbed at Zephyr's mane, tugging him still and maddening him at the same time. He bucked, and I, gripping my shield in one hand and curved bow in the other, slid backwards across his rump and fell onto the bloody sand.

All air fled my body, and I choked like a drowning man, unable to catch my breath. Someone else's blood sprayed across my face and neck—hot and thick with life, for a short time, at least.

Sucking in air, at last, I staggered to my feet. Where was Zephyr? I blinked back the blood from my eyes. There he was, hooves churning up the sands. He reared and kicked a man in the chest, the very man who'd tried to grapple with him and caused me to fall. The soldier fell back, his cuirass deeply dented from the horse's hooves, and onto the ground, unmoving. Zephyr lashed his hooves at another soldier before turning to search for me. I reached out my shield hand, but before I could grab him and remount, a large shadow loomed over me.

"Time to die, little girl," came a booming voice over my shoulder.

I spun immediately, striking this new attacker with the edge of my bow. Though it was wood, I managed to hit him across the throat, and he staggered back, gasping. I stared at him, sizing him up, while he recovered and flexed his bulging muscles.

A mountain of a man stood before me now. I recognized him vaguely as the slayer of Priam's two sons earlier in the battle. Some Argive hero, some champion, empowered because of his great size and greater thirst for blood. We were all heroes, I thought, and all monsters, for our heroism, always shared bloodlust and endless murders. I sighed though the battle rang thick around me. I had hoped to find Achilles in all this, hoped to fight with honor, perhaps die with it too — but now this great monster stood before me, sword glistening wet with blood and eyes dark coals within the depths of his helm.

"Ajax!" cried a voice. Achilles. He charged from the other end of the battlefield towards us. "Ajax, she is mine to fight!"

The Argive warrior before me only laughed and slashed at me with the point of his spear. I thwacked it away with the flat of my shield before it could pierce my cuirass. Ajax, as Achilles had named him, bore down on me, moving faster than expected for such a large man. His sword, the blade of which was broader than my arm, chopped down and down, and I could only dodge so fast to get out of its path. Laughing as I dodged his blows, his teeth glowed like little pearls in his dark face. I swung my shield up to deflect another blow — but when he struck, my arm jarred painfully all the way up to my shoulder.

I staggered back, feet slipping in the sand.

Ajax flicked the butt of his javelin and sent it sweeping against my hip. Pain. Pain shot down my leg, and I fell to one side. Had he broken any bones? I could feel nothing but fire. My bow slipped from my hand. I fumbled for the hilt of my sword, wrenching it free from its scabbard at my side. I clenched my teeth and felt hot blood in my mouth from where I must have bit my tongue in the attack. Ajax lunged. His sword slipped between the crevices in my armor and tore into the skin just below my armpit.

I snarled in anger and scuttled away. Finally, my sword was out. Blood rushed down the wound, but I flew at him, attacking when I knew he expected me to falter. Now he was bringing his sword up in defense, blocking my blows. He was a giant, but I was tall for a woman and fueled by pain—physical, from the wound, and mental, from seeing one by one my sister Amazons fall. Ajax hefted his great, rectangular shield to deflect my strikes. I slunk around to his side, keeping him always turning round and round, forcing him on the defensive. In his anger, he roared like a great cat, took two steps back and then launched his spear. Seeing the bronze point hurtling towards me, I momentarily thought of Hector and how he must have felt seeing the spear of Achilles coming to take his life. But in a flash, I ducked and felt only the jagged spearhead as it tore across my shoulder, drawing a line of blood over my collarbone and tearing the leopard pelt from my back.

"Die, girl!" cried Ajax, clearly enraged that he had barely wounded me.

I slashed my sword across his leg and sliced a deep cut

into his thick thigh muscle. "I'm not a girl," I hissed. "I am a queen."

The giant toppled to one knee, and I turned to scour the rest of the battle. Warriors fell on all sides, including my Amazons, the fighting stronger and more frantic than I had previously seen it here. There were no duels for honor. There was only desperation, clawing hands, hacking weapons, screams, terrible screams. Through the churned-up dust, I could see none of the other Amazons, save Antibrote, who had made it to my side. Like me, she had lost her horse. I hoped—no, prayed—that Zephyr had gotten away safely, one last reminder of Hector safe from the squalid terror of the war.

Then, through the mist and the choking dust appeared Achilles. His black armor was stained with blood and sand, his face invisible within his helmet. He seemed to float rather than walk in my direction, strength and power exuding from the sun-kissed muscles visible on his arms and legs.

"I told Ajax not to fight you," he said, his voice carrying over the crash and racket of the battlefield.

I nodded my head towards him in acknowledgement. "I fight any man who attacks from now until the day I die," I replied.

Achilles threw his spear. It cracked against the moon shape of my shield with such power that half of it broke away, leaving me with a crescent to protect myself. I threw off broken shards of shield and charged. So did Achilles, and our swords met with a ring that could be heard back in Priam's palace. We both reeled back from the force of the blows but quickly launched ourselves again and again. Each thwack of blade against shield alternated with a killing lunge. But our weapons never made contact, never sliced through muscle, never tore into bone. Achilles and I whirled around each other, not with the ease of dancers but the simplicity of being so evenly matched.

I could think of only one other fighter who had been my equal, and that was Hector. I panted, my throat raw from the constant effort. Hector and I and Achilles — and Hippolyta — we were all the same, soldiers taught to perform feats of war. And we were taught well. I dodged a blow from Achilles that might have snapped my leg in half. Anchises had taught us here in Ilium. Achilles himself had learned somewhere back in the lands of the Argives. We had all learned so well.

I threw my head back and laughed before thumping my shield into Achilles' chest. How funny it seemed, how absurd that we had spent all our lives learning to kill and fight. Why? So we could die on the rotten plains in front of a dying city? So we could be heroes, spoken and sung of in ballads and legends? Did it matter that I had cried over my first kill, the dangerous, beautiful cat — that I still cried over it sometimes in quiet moments? Did it matter that Achilles would never smile again now that his dear Patroclus, another warrior, had followed our one and only path? Did it matter that poor Andromache and Hecuba would never recover from the loss of Hector and that he had only died because some stupid morality kept us all fighting each other for any little slight?

And did it matter that Helen, who had supposedly started the whole war by going off with Paris, had not wanted to be married to Menelaus in the first place? So why did he fight so hard to take her back? Why did we all fight so hard for something that meant so little?

Achilles' breath grew labored, but still, he spun out of grasp at every turn. I could see nothing of his face or expression beneath his helmet, but I wondered if he shared the same thoughts. The futility, the waste of it all, caught my breath. Had I ever taken pleasure in warfare? Had I ever thought I enjoyed this life? All I wanted at that moment was to ride with Zephyr, to fly free from the constant war and bloodshed, to race against the winds and rejoice in the sky and sea and sun.

Achilles, my great enemy, my nemesis in this war, shot forwards with his sword. It sundered my armor and pierced the flesh of my belly. I gasped.

My body, the strong, fighting form of the Queen of the Amazons, fell to the sands.

Chapter 18 - απελπισία

DESPAIR

Hippolyta's blood ran through my fingers and down my wrists. Blood burbled from her lips and spilled down her chin. When she looked up at me, her teeth were all painted red.

"No!" I cried. "Lyta!"

"Sister…." she sputtered, but her eyes were already growing pale, the light in them dimming until she slid down the edge of my sword and slumped to the ground.

My hands shook. My body ached as if I were the one dead. Women's hands came to me then, claimed me when I could not move myself. There were words, cries, shouts, whispers—I did not know, and I did not care. My Lyta was gone. My dear, dear Lyta.

The world around me blurred as if a fog had risen. And indeed, the fog of my despair clouded almost everything from my view. All I could see were my hands, my blood-covered hands, and the sword I still held in them. Why was it not my blood? Why was I not the one slain?

Sometime later, I awoke. Hunger thrummed in my belly,

but I refused to eat. The Amazons wrapped me in cloaks and offered me water. From the constant rocking, I assumed we were on a ship. One of our ships? Fleeing Athens and returning to Themyscira? I could not know. Our path was not drawn out in the dried blood caked on my hands, so I could not see it.

My heart ached for days, then it curled in on itself, becoming stone, a block of iron in my chest.

Without Lyta, there was no reason to love. There was no reason to live.

Then a hand was reaching for my cheek, caressing my sweat and tear-stained face.

"Oh, Pen," said a voice.

I shifted my eyes dully. Through the blood and haze, I thought I recognized the face of my mother. The real queen of the Amazons, not the one who had accidentally slain her own sister.

Otrera gathered me in her arms, older and weaker than I remembered. "Pen, dear Pen," she said over and over. Together we rocked back and forth. I felt nothing. "Pen, you did not mean it. It wasn't your intention."

"Is that why you told me not to go?" I asked, my voice a small croak in the back of my throat. "Did you foresee this as you foresaw Artemis' temple?"

My mother shook her head and tucked my dark, dirty curls behind one ear. "No, Pen. But I thought it was a mistake, even then. I knew you should not have interfered with Lyta's life."

I pulled away from her. "But he was going to abandon her! Mother, he left her for some other girl. She would never have been happy with him, whether I came or not." Why could she not see? Why could she not make more sense of all this?

My vision faded. My mother was gone, and I stared up at the temple before me, the one Otrera had left us to build. A little wooden building set behind a tree.

This. This was what she'd abandoned us to dedicate. I felt hate and bile surge through me. I hated my mother for leaving us for some stupid building, some temple that meant less than the trees and a prayer sung to the moon on a winter night. I hated Hippolyta for being so stupid as to trust King Theseus.

And I hated myself for submitting to my rage and for killing her, though it had been an accident.

The stone of my heart grew colder still. I was a killer. The Queen of Killers. I was covered in my sister's blood, and I myself deserved nothing less than sorrow and death. I curled into myself before the wretched temple of the Moon Goddess, burying the pain under rage and the despair under seething fury. I would die—no, I would bring death to others, those deserving of it as I was. I would fight and kill and battle until my own blood drained away.

Chapter 19 - πόλεμος

THE WAR

Blood seeped from my wound in a trickle, then a torrent. My muscles twitched and grew cold. Perhaps it had finally come. The death I'd hoped for for so long.

Achilles knelt beside me. He tore off his helmet, then mine. His light eyes searched mine, his brow furrowed, sweat dripping down it.

"Penthesilea?" His voice was low, almost a whisper.

I stared up at him, feeling my body weaken. I stared into his blue eyes, the same clear blue of the sky above him.

And I wanted to live.

I thought of the trees on Themyscira, the little rivers crisscrossing it, the hot sands of its beaches beneath my bare feet. I thought of my hand on Zephyr's flank and feeling the life pump elegantly through his body.

And my grief for Hippolyta slid from me like a discarded pall.

I wanted to live. I wanted to live without killing, without warring, without battling men for no reason.

"I want to live," I gasped, my eyes locking with Achilles'.

He placed his hands on either side of my face and stroked my cheeks. Tears formed in the corners of his eyes, just beside the little creases and wrinkles that had begun there.

"Oh gods, Penthesilea," he said. "You, out of us all, you deserve most to live."

The tears dripped from his eyes and down his nose into my face. I blinked them away from my own eyes.

"Close your eyes, Pen," he said, using a nickname he could not have known. "Close your eyes, and let me end this. You will be at peace."

Peace, I thought. I closed my eyes. The trees of my island filled my view. Waving leaves and threading branches. Peace—peace was home. Peace was Zephyr. Peace was life.

I waited for another blow from Achilles' sword, the final blow.

But it did not come.

My face burned in the sun, and I squinted through one eye. Achilles rose and turned his back on me. Then he strode through the mess of corpses and picked up something from amongst them. My leopard pelt torn from my body during the fight with Ajax. He lifted it tenderly and placed it over a nearby body.

I stared blankly at the body staring back at me. My leopard pelt lay upon the body of Antibrote, now dead and eyes glazed. In the bright sunlight, I again was struck with how much she looked like me. What did Achilles intend?

And then his voice cut across the battlefield. "Here lies Penthesilea," he cried, "Queen of the Amazons. A worthy fighter and a worthier friend. Take her body, men of Ilium. See that it has all the honors of a hero."

The fighting had stilled all around us. Men and warriors

stopped their killing and their struggling and listened to Achilles.

And so I was dead but not dead. They honored the body of Antibrote as if she were me.

After the soldiers straggled away, I fingered the wound in my gut. It was bloody, but perhaps not deadly, not as deep as I had thought. Achilles had spared me.

Because I asked him to live?

No, because we were the same and because he also wanted to live. Not to avenge Patroclus or Hippolyta but to honor them.

When the sun fell, but before the corpse-gatherers came, I rose. I discarded my sword and armor and strode, not towards Ilium but to the northeast. Ilium was doomed, and I had done as much as I could. We all had. It was a little walk to the beach, but there I sank my feet into the cool waters.

A familiar neigh greeted me. I spun around to find a golden face burying itself in mine.

"Zephyr!" I cried, and I wrapped my arms around his neck, feeling his head and shoulders for signs of injury. He was well, or at least as well as I was.

I held him crushed in my arms for a moment before swinging back up into his saddle. The leather felt good, familiar to me, though I had no wish to charge into battle as we had often done.

"Come, Zephyr," I said, and kicked him gently. Together we ambled along the coast, northeast, always northeast. Eventually, we would reach the island. Eventually, we would be home.

Otrera named me Penthesilea, or "mourned by men." And mourned by many I would be — by Achilles for as long as his short life burned brightly in his breast, by Aeneas in his stories to his little son, by my mother who would hear of our defeat at Ilium. Would she shed a tear for me? Would she pray in her temple to Artemis, a deity nearly unrecognizable to me as my beloved Moon Goddess? And, for a little while at least, I would be mourned by myself. The Penthesilea who once was. But I was a new Pen, a new woman, turning ever towards the sun and the wind and to life.

Acknowledgments

Writing a book is such a bizarre experience. You pour your heart into a character and a world so different from your own, only to be left wondering, did I really do that? That can't be right. I'm not cool enough to do that. I still can't quite believe that something I wrote is out there in the world.

To Karen Fuller and everyone at World Castle who believed in my work, your trust has meant everything to me. Thank you for taking a chance on me and Penthesilea.

So many teachers and professors have shaped my love of writing, literature, and mythology. Enormous thanks to Janet Ross, who taught me to diagram sentences (still a weirdly fun activity), and the late Rosemary Powers, who stoked my interest in writing way back in first grade. Of course, I also thank my high school Latin teacher, Dennis Gaynor, as well as Anthony Millspaugh and Gregory Vecchio, for their literary encouragement.

I also want to thank so many professors at Loyola University, especially Dr. James Biester, as well as the Classics Department. I can't thank these amazing scholars enough: Dr. John Makowski (whose dramatic recitations always dazzle), Dr. Brian Lavelle, Dr. Penny Livermore (an actual bright star in the firmament of education), Dr. Pat Graham-Skoul (thank you for pointing me towards Adrienne Mayor's book The Amazons!), and the late Dr. Gregory Dobrov, who brought so much laughter and joy into the classroom. Any liberties or inconsistencies in this retelling are solely mine.

My own family, who has put up with my dramatic antics forever—thank you for understanding my madness and encouraging me in this and all my endeavors. Thank you, found family, Danny and Penelope, for cheering me on/sassing me, and to Bettina Maravolo for reading and supporting my work even though we're not related. And thank you to my father. I would not be the writer I am without your inimitable narrative abilities. To Mike, thank you for putting up with my perpetual messiness and my dreams.

To my canine best friends, I thank Pacey for being a lovable angel, and the late Daisy, for sitting on my computers/notebooks whenever I tried to write.

And to Joey and my mom, thank you both for always reading what I write. So many words and so much enthusiasm. It means the world.

Katie Frendreis grew up in Chicago, reading mythology and illustrating her own fantastical adventures. This is her first published novel. She earned her BA in Classical Civilization from Loyola University and has worked in such diverse places as museums, dance studios, and funeral homes. Collecting hobbies like some people collect stamps, she also draws, paints, teaches tap dancing, and trains as an aerialist. She currently lives just outside Chicago with her husband, a massive collection of books, and a rather large Lego community in her basement.

Printed in the USA
CPSIA information can be obtained
at www.ICGtesting.com
LVHW091810201123
764459LV00001B/2

9 781960 076946